HARD ROADS

HARD ROADS

Steve Vernon

HARD ROADS

First published in 2007 by Gray Friar Press.
19 Ruffield Side, Delph Hill, Wyke, Bradford,
West Yorkshire, BD12 8DP, England.

Email: g.fry@blueyonder.co.uk
www.grayfriarpress.com

Typesetting by Gary Fry and Simon Strantzas

ISBN:
0955092280 paperback limited to 300 copies
0955092299 hardback limited to 100 copies

CONTENTS

Down The Road A Piece
An Introduction by
Norman Partridge
i

Trolling Lures
3

Hammurabi Road
91

Dedication

To my brother, Danny Vernon, who told me about railroading from the inside out; and never let me down.

To my wife Belinda, as always, you are the guiding star this here tale-telling gypsy steers his heart by.

Note

These two novellas are the first stories I've written that take place in my home ground of Nova Scotia and my birth place of Northern Ontario and all I can say is it's good to come home, no matter how long or hard the road was to get here.

DOWN THE ROAD A PIECE

Norman Partridge

When you walk the writer's road, you get to know a lot of people you've never met.

That's the way it is with me and Steve Vernon. I've never met Steve, never spent a minute in his company or even talked to him on the phone, but I've "known" him for years through his writing. Hey, we had stories back to back in *Cemetery Dance* #2, and if you know anything about horror you know that one rolled off the presses many, many moons ago.

Yep. In those days, Rich Chizmar was a young guy fresh out of college and writers were just beginning to transition from typewriters to those new-fangled "home computers." With its fat Macintosh dot-matrix type and rock-and-chisel design, *CD* wasn't much to look at back then. As a publisher, Rich was learning by doing. As writers, Steve and I were doing the same, publishing stories that had more than a little rough on 'em. The horror small press was beginning to seriously crank its gears, and we took advantage of that by getting our work out there in little markets that were hustling to find an audience. That's where we sharpened our skills as storytellers. At the same time, we were looking for opportunities in the larger professional anthology markets…and – when we weren't banging away on stories – we were also thinking about writing novels that could bust through with a New York publisher.

Of course, Steve had gotten a little bit of a jump on me. *CD* #2 was my first publication, while our buddy Mr. Vernon had been cashing checks from publishers for several years. He started off writing for motorcycle magazines in the eighties, and after a couple detours in mystery, fantasy, and (surprise!) even romance, he jumped to horror. That's where Steve's work really took root, and he started to rack up a good list of sales. His stories appeared in such bygone 'zines as *After Hours*, *October Dreams*, *Terror Time Again*, and *The Horror Show*. And, yes, I've got to send curses Steve's way for the latter sale, as I never could crack Dave Silva's much-praised magazine. Damn you, Steve Vernon!

Anyway, barring the mouthful of sour grapes just choked down by yours truly, let me tell you it was an exciting time to break in to the horror biz. A lot of new writers were appearing on the table of contents pages of magazines like the ones listed above. Some of them weren't so good, and some of them were damned good. A lot of the good ones made the jump into pro anthologies, and it wasn't long before stories from those little 'zines began to crack the *Year's Best* anthologies for short fiction. Steve himself made it into Karl Edward Wagner's annual compilation...and, yeah, Wagner's was the one *Year's Best* series I never cracked. (Hey...can you pass me those grapes? I could use a few more. Thanks.)

But it's a funny thing about writing, and about writing careers. Folks who give it a try never realize what a long road it's going to be, and there aren't too many who stick with it. Or to put it another way: there were plenty of writers I shared space with in those little magazines who I figured I'd be reading for years...and some of them I did. But most of them? It was one or two stories and *thanks for the memories, pard.* They put writing in the rearview and found themselves another road, maybe one that was well-paved and easy to navigate...two things the writing road definitely ain't.

A lot of times it's just like that. Some writers get the itch to be published, and it goes away nearly as soon as their name hits ink and they get their first little scratch. Others see their creative fire doused by a bucket of cold reality. The writing business certainly provides a steady supply of those. But for some, that road keeps on calling no matter what. Sometimes the going's fast and sure and bullet-straight, sometimes it's switchbacks and gravel and potholes, but its call endures, and those who answer it make the trip with fingers on a keyboard, driving words across the page, going that extra mile…and maybe one more after that.

Most of us would like to think we're that kind of writer. It's a hard call to make, especially if you're looking at yourself. But Steve fits the bill. He's stuck to the road, with hard work and good work. He's told stories on paper, and he's spun them with words as a professional oral-tradition storyteller, and he's done both things for a good long time now.

Yep. Mr. Vernon's come down that road a piece. And I'm sure he's discovered that one of the great things about sticking to it is that it changes over the course of the writer's journey, and the writer – if he's lucky – changes right along with it.

I've seen that in my own work over the years, and I've seen it in Steve's, too. See, I remember Steve's early stories. I remember "In Loving Memory" in *Cemetery Dance* #2. I remember "Mongrel" in *CD* #5. And while those were both good pieces, they were the kind of stories we all write when we're starting out. Solid and steady if we're lucky, and they'll deliver us (and the reader) to the appointed destination. But in a lot of ways they're like making a trip in another guy's car. Sure, it'll get you where you're going, but it's not *your* car…and there's a difference in that. There really is.

With *Hard Roads*, we're definitely in Steve Vernon's car. He's the guy behind the wheel. He knows just where we're going, and he's not about to spare the horses. I've seen the signs of that coming for a while now. *Long Horn, Big Shaggy*, Steve's recent weird western, melded his storytelling voice with a little Lansdale and a little Brautigan. It came out all aces. It was great fun, and one of the best reads I've had in recent memory. But this one's different. There are no backseat drivers here. Steve owns these stories, just as he owns this landscape. With *Hard Roads* we're on his home turf, Nova Scotia, a patch of Canada that – up to now – he hasn't explored outside his work in the oral (and folkloric) tradition.

Believe me, that's one thing that really puts the pedal to the metal in these stories. It fires them up, and it fires Steve up, too. I'll spare you any blurbage here, or any hype. Stories like "Trolling Lures" and "Hammurabi Road" don't need that. They just flatout burn up some roadbed all on their own. You're about to find that out.

While you're at it, a word of warning: it might be a good idea to fasten your seatbelt. The ride is sure to be just a little bumpy, and these are the kind of stories that might just leave some skidmarks on your brain. And that guy behind the wheel? Watch out for him. I've got a feeling he'll get you where *he's* going…but like the title says, these are hard roads you'll be traveling, and I can't guarantee you'll make the trip in one piece.

Norman Partridge
Lafayette, California,
June 2, 2007

TROLLING LURES

They call me Troll;
Gnawer of the Moon
Giant of the Gale-blasts,
Curse of the rain-hall,
Companion of the Sibyl,
Nightroaming beast,
Swallower of the loaf of heaven.
What is a troll but that?
(taken from the Eda, an ancient Norse poem
by Bragi Boddason)

The forest is where all maps end
and all possibilities begin
(old Mi'kmaq saying)

Prologue

The boy trembled in the tight darkness, waiting for the trapdoor to swing open. He knew he'd be beaten. He heard the troll's footsteps thumping like rocks against the floorboards. He crouched and curled like a pill bug in the darkness.

"Help me god, help me god, help me god, help me…" Over and over, a tightly whispered prayer bleeding into litany. "God help me god help me."

The footsteps hammered closer. God, it seemed, wasn't listening.

The sliver of light that marked the edge of the trapdoor widened. The boy blinked against the sudden brightness. The trapdoor swung open. A face looked down. At least he was wearing the father mask.

"You lose her?" the troll rumbled.

The boy nodded.

"Why?"

"She was thirsty. I tried to give her a drink. The cup wouldn't fit through the willow bars, so I opened her cage. She flew like a bird right out of the cage."

"How'd she slip the chain?"

"She pulled it off. She left some skin behind."

"Come on," the troll said.

The boy clambered eagerly out from his hiding spot. He knew better than to ask questions. He followed the troll to the truck and climbed on to the back.

"She'll head for the road," the troll said. "We'll pick her trail up there. Put your chain on. We're going fishing."

The sun was shining but the boy trembled harder because fishing was worse than a beating.

He put the chain on, like a dog, eager for the leash. While he was doing that he noticed a coyote squatting on the verge of the camp.

The troll saw the coyote too.

"Are you going to give me trouble?" the troll asked, fixing the coyote with an evil dark eye.

The coyote wagged his wild bushy tail and promptly sicked up his last meal.

#

CHAPTER 1
The Running Girl

Morgan Hillman leaned out of his parked Volvo and puked. The mess splattered hot and funky upon the gravel of the roadside.

"You stink like a mile of dead skunks," the dead woman said.

Hillman mustered a fart that he knew would streak his skivvies. It hurt coming out, same as the puke. Cancer did that to a man.

"Smell that," he said to the dead woman. That was the good thing about being haunted. You didn't have to bother being polite to phantoms.

He wiped his mouth and managed a smile. With cancer gnawing in his belly, thoughts of suicide percolating in his brain, and the spirit-memory of a dead woman in the backseat of his Volvo station wagon, he figured it was a damned good day to die.

He looked down at the mess in the gravel. There they were. Chopped carrots. It seemed like no matter what he ate there were always some chopped carrots in the mess that came back up. He couldn't even remember the last time he'd eaten chopped carrots.

"Are you on the right road?" the dead woman asked.

Hillman looked up at the road sign. It read 106.

"It's the road I'm on," he said, cranking the key and

nudging the gas.

The dead woman had been with him for as long as he could remember. He didn't know if she was real or not. He could see and hear her. She was beautiful in the haunting way that native women often are. The cave of her skull, opened by a .38 caliber skeleton key, writhed with a glitter of maggots. On the unmarked side of her face a single dark eye stared out, frozen like a shard of broken green glass. As delusions went, he'd painted her up in a fine old style.

The Volvo thundered over a heavy iron bridge, heading west down the 106. The radio spoke of clearing skies, high temperatures, and a chance of rain. Hillman smiled. It was perfect weather for the end of the world – absolutely undecided.

"Have you got enough nerve for this?" the dead woman asked.

"Just watch me," Hillman said.

How fast a world can end, he thought. It seemed like yesterday he stood at a Halifax lunch counter, serving out coffee. Now look at him. Driving down a Nova Scotia rural highway, counting off the minutes until self-extinction.

"I know who you are," the dead woman said.

"I wish I knew who you were," Hillman replied.

He couldn't remember when he'd started seeing her. She'd been with him for as long as he recalled. Delusions followed that sort of pattern. Like a nervous habit, you were never quite sure just when they started. One day you were normal, the next you found yourself talking to invisible gods and sticking your tongue out, Maori-style, every time you heard the mention of Paris Hilton's name.

The landscape slipped past like an unspooling movie reel. The early October sunshine, determined to make the most of these last few weeks of heat, cast shadows darker than burned black. Patches of rolling dry thatch mixed with bursts of third growth forest. Great joints of granite thrust up from the soil. Leaves hung grimly upon heat-withered branches, their colors running from vivid green into the gasoline of autumn, ready to flutter into mulch like a legion of moldering paratroopers.

A portion of Hillman's waking mind appreciated the stark beauty, but a deeper part of himself absently listened to the sound of Big Billy Tumor clawing his finest fiddle bow, deep within the windings of Hillman's gut. Big Billy Tumor was a hungry little booger. He never stopped eating at Hillman's insides, turning the cells one by one.

"Who is nibbling on my house?" Hillman ruefully muttered. "Who is nibbling like a mouse?"

He bounced along the road in his black Volvo station wagon, praying that the suspension would live up to the abuse, keeping half an eye on the photocopied map that he'd taped to his dashboard. He'd highlighted his chosen route in black marker with a bright red X designating his end destination. It was good to know where he was going to die. He'd mapped everything out to the very last detail. Careful plans were a lonely man's final form of prayer.

He traveled light. A fiberglass fishing rod, a bright red tackle box, a haversack stuffed with a couple of tins of beans and beef jerky sticks, a creel and a net.

"Who do you think you're fooling? Insurance companies never pay off on suicides," the dead woman taunted. "You're living in a web of lies, spun by yourself."

She was wrong. He would fool them. His camouflage was perfect, right down to the battered fishing hat and the many-pocketed camp vest. It was hunting season. No one would question the presence of the shotgun stowed behind the seat.

"What do you need insurance money for anyway?"

What indeed, Hillman wondered. He didn't have anyone to leave anything to. He wouldn't be missed.

Somebody else could easily make a better cup of coffee.

Why was he doing it this way?

He didn't have a clue. A few slices of truth lay stuffed in the brown manila envelope resting on the passenger seat. A handwritten prognosis and the X-rays that he'd grabbed from the doctor's office. He'd burn the note and the envelope and the X-ray photographs in his campfire, make his peace with the world, and then go out into the woods and find a fence to tangle up in while crossing over. An accidental discharge. It happened all of the time. He'd checked the statistics.

He wondered where the dead woman would go. Would she find someone else to haunt? Or maybe she'd just linger over his carcass as he forgot himself back into the dirt.

His stomach made sounds like a bubbling cauldron. Big Billy Tumor gnawed into his viscera like a multi-mouthed worm working in the darkness. He felt his cells playing Star Wars games, one by one surrendering to the dark side.

That's how cancer worked. The doctor had explained it. A single cell wakes up one morning and decides it doesn't like the way it's been growing. It was the ultimate midlife crisis. The man inside the man tried to work his way out, cell by cell. The escape artist, mutating in a misguided attempt to remake his very being.

"Nibble, nibble, have some kibbles."

Cancer – the original clone wars. It was funny how funny it seemed. The walking dead tell the best jokes. The doctor spelled Hillman's obituary out in a handful of dirty multi-syllable words.

"Malignant. Terminal. Inoperable," the dead woman taunted. "Give yourself time. You'll look as bad as I do. The shotgun will be an improvement."

"I heard his words," Hillman said. He wasn't bothered by the diagnosis, any more than he was bothered by talking to the spirit of a dead woman. It was easy to accept a lot of things when you knew you were going to die.

He wasn't alarmed anymore. He felt peaceful, like watching a forensic medical show on the television. How fast can a body decay?

Death happened to everyone, sooner or later. There was really no need to get upset. The old croupier had reached out and raked Hillman's chips a little closer to the bank. It was time to cash out.

"I'll wait for you over there, on the other side of the bridge," the dead woman taunted. "Death's no escape for the likes of you."

"What'd I ever do to you to earn such an honor?"

"You'll remember," the dead woman said.

"Is that a prayer, a promise, or a threat?"

He wondered again where she'd come from. He knew she belonged to him, the same as the cancer.

He wondered if the cancer knew what he was up to. If the malignant growth suspected that its host might somehow terminally interrupt its long slow feast.

"Sing Hallelujah, Big Billy. The anvil chorus is about to drop on your head."

Big Billy was the name that Hillman had given his tumor. It made the whole thing kind of friendly, like death was nothing more than a permanent pass-out drunk-up with a really good buddy. Hillman thought of his cancer with the face of a mutated Billy Graham painted across its septic features, preaching faster as the end came on, a sub-molecular televangelist trying to convert each cell.

Hillman closed his eyes. For a half an instant he saw the woman and the gun going off. Him standing there, just watching like it was television.

"Why did you shoot?" the dead woman wanted to know.

In the reruns of his endlessly broadcasting

imagination, Hillman saw the coffee shop, the door opening wide like a mouth, the jingle bells hung on the door ringing...

"*Look out!*" the dead woman shouted.

Hillman snapped open his eyes, jarred from his reverie just in time to see the coyote leap in front of his Volvo. His fist was already hard down on the horn, working it instinctively.

He twisted the wheel, veering straight into the path of the running girl.

#

CHAPTER 2
The Laws of Dead Children and Murdered Spirits

Hillman hit the brakes too late. There was a thump, like a period at the end of a death sentence. A flash of color lofted across his windshield, not quite fast enough for him not to have seen exactly what he'd done.

The Volvo fishtailed across the roadway, coming to a halt just beyond where he'd collided with the girl. Hillman fumbled with the seat belt, cursing himself for even bothering buckling it in the first place. Whose life had he been trying to save?

The girl's body lay in the gravel of the roadside. Damn. She couldn't have been more than sixteen. Her body was bent in too many directions to be still living. A single black pigtail shot out from her head, the other braid splayed open from the impact. He'd hit her that hard. He saw the bright red elastic from her unbound braid lying about six feet away from her broken skull.

Her left leg twisted backwards. Shattered femur, he thought, although he couldn't figure out how he knew that.

Where had he learned this, he wondered?

She lay flat upon the roadside, her face a smashed pudding from where it had bounced. Her neck was broken. Her head was completely turned around, as if she'd died looking over her shoulder.

He picked her up as gently as he could. He knew he was disturbing the scene of a crime. He knew he was breaking every rule of first aid. What did it matter? The little girl was dead and he was going to kill himself. How many more laws could he break?

She felt so heavy for so young a girl. Broken and wet in places she shouldn't ought to be.

There was a mark on her ankle. It looked deeper than an injury. The skin on her foot was torn off, peeled like it had been flensed. There'd been iron, some kind of a bracelet, only heavier than a bracelet. The chaffing was far too deep for any mere decoration.

Manacles. That's what it looked like. The girl had been shackled in some sort of leg irons. He leaped to the conclusion like a man leaping onto a running train.

What had he stumbled into? He couldn't call for help. He didn't want to and even if he did, he didn't have a cell phone with him. He didn't believe in them. There were times when a man just needed to be alone.

Like when he was killing himself.

He leaned her body against the side of the Volvo. She nearly slid downwards. He'd expected her to support herself. Stupid. She was dead. She was long past standing up for herself.

He leaned there against her, breathing as if he'd run a ragged mile. He'd driven this far thinking of his death, but at the age of 53 that just didn't seem as important a loss as death grabbing someone as young as this girl.

He opened the side door of the Volvo and laid her body in. The dead woman made room for the girl's body, as if she'd been expecting company.

The little girl fit into the back seat easily. Hillman wondered if there wasn't some sort of law of physics governing the placing of dead teenagers and murdered spirits into the passenger end of a Volvo station wagon.

What could he do? This would spoil his plans. She was dead. Who had done this? He knew he was responsible for hitting her, but there had to have been somebody else responsible for her being out here in the first place.

What could he do? Hunt the bastard down? What chance did he have of finding him? He didn't even know if it was a him or not. It could easily have been a woman. Child abuse wasn't strictly the province of male offenders.

Male offenders. He laughed at the phrase. He'd been watching too many police shows. He was beginning to sound as if he knew what he was talking about.

He looked across the road. The coyote was still standing there.

"Do you smell dead meat? Is that what you want, you bastard?"

Hillman bent and picked up a rock. The coyote didn't move. Hillman wanted to hit the beast. If he hadn't been swerving to avoid the coyote, he might have seen the girl in time.

"Go on," he hollered at the coyote.

The coyote looked anxiously down the road.

"Go on," Hillman hollered, not wanting to throw the rock. He hated abusing animals.

The coyote fixed him with a lasered yellow stare.

"You better get in your car," the coyote said. "He's coming."

Hillman gawked. The coyote had spoken, moving his lips around the words like he'd known what he was saying. He touched his skull, wondering about the possibility of concussion.

"He's coming fast," the coyote warned. "Too late

now."

Then Hillman heard the roar coming far too fast. He looked down the road and saw it coming.

The big red truck aimed straight for him.

#

CHAPTER 3

Cocked, Locked and Ready To Roar

The big red Ford pickup truck nearly impacted against Hillman's Volvo, cutting him off and bulling ahead with a loud blast of horn music. It roared up to the top of the rise ahead and then braked to a halt with a screech of smoldering tires. The truck waited there, gunning its engine.

Stupid macho redneck bastard.

Then Hillman saw the boy, riding in the back of the truck.

He thought it was a dog at first. You see a lot of that in the country. Labrador retrievers and rabbit hounds bouncing around in the bed of a pickup truck along with beer cases, two by fours, and several balding spare tires.

Only this wasn't a dog. It was a boy. He looked about ten or twelve years old and even from this distance he looked scared shitless.

Hillman couldn't blame him. It was cold and scary up on a truck if you weren't up for it. And ten or twelve years was a long way from up for anything in Hillman's books.

Damn backwoods trailer park cowboys. Didn't they know anything about safety?

Never mind. It wasn't any of his business.

He got back into the Volvo. He had enough of his own problems. What could he do with the girl?

And then he noticed the glint of the chain and the steel collar, bound like a noose about the boy's thin white throat. The kid was chained to the truck. Damn. This was the bastard who'd done the girl. It had to be.

"Jumping to conclusions, aren't you?" the dead woman asked.

"I haven't got time for debate."

Hillman jammed his boot down hard against the gas pedal. He wasn't sure what he was going to do yet, but he knew there was no way he could sit here and do nothing. He'd done nothing once before, and had ended up with blood on his hands.

When? When had that happened?

There was no time now for introspection. The truck had started up as well.

Hillman accelerated, working the wheel, thinking Steve McQueen Bullitt fantasies, while living in the reality-cage of Buddy Hackett's Love Bug. He was no stunt car driver.

The pick up was a distant red crawl, getting fatter by the minute as the Volvo gained on it. Hillman figured he could catch it. He bounced the heavy Volvo over a pothole. Damned Nova Scotia roads. What the hell did he pay taxes for?

"Fuckhead hot air politicians!" he shouted, letting the words roll like pent up thunder. "May you filibuster forever in an election hall filled with deaf blind nonvoters!"

Then he grinned for the very first time since he'd heard the doctor's prognosis. Hell, it was the first time in a long time that he'd felt alive.

What kind of sense did that make? Feeling alive on the day of his suicide. That was fate for you. A universal whoopee cushion. God was a fat ball-capped asshole with a wicked wet sense of humor.

The tires squealed as he fought the car around a

wide turn. Slow it down. You can't save the boy if you kill yourself.

Save the boy. When had his plan become that? He'd come out here to kill himself. He'd had it all figured out. What was he thinking now? He wasn't sure.

Fuck it. He'd done a lot of things in the last few years without needing to know why.

"Save the boy," he whispered aloud. Why not? He had nothing to lose. What was the worst that could happen? He would run the truck off of the road and shoot the driver. Orphan the boy and set him free. Give him the keys to the truck and send him on home. Hillman would still have time to ventilate his own skull before dinner.

It sounded reasonable if you thought it out fast.

"Save the boy," the dead woman echoed from the back seat. The dead girl, rocking against the dead woman, said nothing.

He was closer now. Tailgating the bastard. He could see the boy, hanging on in the truck bed. He must have been tied in some how to hold on at this speed. What if he fell off?

Hillman goosed the gas a little harder. He might have told himself to be careful, but that was stupid. How do you carefully run a pick-up truck off of the road with a Volvo?

He had to try. He pulled up along side of the truck. Cruising down the wrong side of the road. If someone was coming in the other direction he'd be killed.

So what?

He saw the driver of the pick-up. A big bastard of a man, judging by the set of his shoulders. The big bastard turned and looked straight at Hillman, ignoring the road. He had a big flat face that looked like it had been painted on. He wore a dark red hunting cap, the color of fresh spilled blood. Big and high with flaps about the ears, the kind of cap Elmer Fudd used to wear. Grown men usually looked a little foolish wearing such caps, but this big bastard didn't look foolish. This big bastard looked dangerous.

"Pull over!" Hillman shouted.

Wasted breath. It was a stupid thing to say, but he'd had to say something.

The big bastard laughed out loud. Hillman couldn't hear the laugh, but he sure could see it. A big smash mouthed hee-haw-haw of a laugh, designed to simultaneously piss off and intimidate.

Hillman thought about his shotgun. Should he pull it out? Wave it? What if the big bastard had a gun too? What if his gun was bigger than Hillman's?

The big bastard sped up. Hillman matched his speed.

"Pull over, damn it!" That was better. Swearing gave him authority, didn't it?

Fuck it. This was stupid. Who did he think he was, Chuck Norris? This wasn't accomplishing anything. His indecision was going to get the boy killed.

For an instant Hillman was back in his coffee shop, standing at the counter staring at the man with the gun.

Then the big bastard stared hard at Hillman. Driving eighty miles an hour and staring like his eyes were a pair of shotgun barrels – cocked, locked and ready to roar.

And then the big bastard reached up one hand and lifted his face open like a trapdoor mask.

#

CHAPTER 4
Always Buckle Your Corpses

The thing behind the pick up truck's steering wheel looked like some kind of nightmarish knight of old, tilting his visor for a quick look-see at the battlefield. Tilting its face back for barely a half an instant.

Peekaboo.

Just enough time for Hillman to register on all of those teeth, like a bag filled with bear traps. What the hell was it?

BAM!

Hillman wasn't certain if the truck had swerved, or if he'd drifted his Volvo into the truck's path. They hit hard, the weight of the Volvo and the truck's momentum sideswiping simultaneously with triphammer force.

The steering wheel twisted in Hillman's grip. He tried to hang on, but veered off the road, out of control. He worked the brake pedal, pumping hard until an obliging jack pine brought the Volvo to a coniferous halt. He saw the tree coming, growing up in his field of vision, and then he hit it hard. The window flew at him, jigsawed into several thousand neat geometric shapes.

The airbag mushroomed open. Hillman fought his way clear. The truck rolled on past. Hillman had just enough of a chance to catch one more look at the chained boy in back of the truck, and then the truck eased to a halt again. It sat there and waited. Hillman got his first good look at the truck. One of those old style Fords, all fat and lumpy with tumor-bumps. Rusted and old and mean looking.

Well what was he waiting for? Was he making sure that Hillman was dead?

And then the truck started backing up. Fast. Coming Hillman's way. Christ, the big bastard was going to ram him in reverse.

The Volvo's driver door was jammed from the impact, so Hillman kicked it twice. The door swung open, and Hilllman clambered out. The truck was backing closer. He couldn't get to the shotgun quickly enough. His aim wasn't good enough to risk hitting the boy. He grabbed his tackle box, and as the truck neared he threw the box.

"Catch!" he shouted.

The box bounced twice. The boy nearly fumbled it.

"Grab it," Hillman prayed aloud.

The boy pulled the tackle box into himself, hugging it like a pup rescued from a flooded stream.

Hillman had just enough time to shout out, "Lay a trail!"

Then, as quickly as it had appeared, the truck was gone.

Hilllman surveyed the damage. The big bastard had dented the hell out of the Volvo's side, and the jack pine had given as good as it got, totalling the Volvo's grill. There was nothing savable. The radiator was stove in, the hood crumpled, and the frame most likely twisted beyond repair.

Fuck.

He'd always thought of the Volvo as being so heavy. A freaking tank, yet just like that it had become vulnerable. Broken.

What next? Should he wait for help? Maybe try and flag down a car?

He stood there, staring down the road. The landscape seemed bleaker, the heavy granite watching him, the jack pines leaning out and teasing him. He could hear the distant waves, just a few miles away, beating against the rocks of the shoreline. The wind roused the autumn leaves into a mocking dance, the hillside to the right of the roadway seemed to be inviting him to jump.

Hillman fished the girl's body from out of the back seat. She hadn't been strapped in. Stupid. He should have thought of that. Before pursuing demon driven trucks, always buckle your corpses in.

What *was* that thing? It couldn't have been real. Were they filming a monster movie somewhere near here?

He looked at her in his arms. Her jaw was pushed in from slamming against the front seat. Maybe death softened meat. Her teeth were bit down into her tongue. He left them there. He didn't want her mouth to hang. At least death staunched the bleeding.

"Save the boy," the dead woman said.

She was standing behind him, just a little to his left. He hadn't seen her get out. Maybe hallucinations didn't need door handles to come and go.

"Save him? How in the hell can I do that? I'm just a goddamned coffee clerk."

"I know who you are," the dead woman said.

"And what the hell does that have to do with anything?"

"Save the boy."

"I can't leave her."

"As you wish. Save the boy."

"Why should I listen to you? You're not even real?"

"*He* is. And he needs your help."

"You sound a Unicef commercial. Go haunt the late late show."

"Those children are far away. This one is near."

Hillman picked the girl up. She was light enough. Could he run with her?

Fuck it.

He set her back down. He leaned through the window into the back seat. The car seemed hot and tainted. He could smell gasoline. It worried him a bit, but not much. Even if the car exploded, the chances of a forest fire were pretty slim. The trees were too wet and green this time of year.

Besides, given his original intention, what would it matter if the car exploded around him?

Well, that kid wouldn't be saved, for one thing.

Hillman fished out the shotgun and slung it over his shoulder. He grabbed the supply pack and slung that over his other shoulder. He had some loose ammo in the glove compartment. He pocketed it.

Stocked and ready, Hillman bent to pick up the dead girl.

Picking up dead teenagers is hard work, but she seemed to slide into his arms, almost making herself comfortable.

"Save the boy," the dead woman repeated.

"You're damned right," Hillman answered.

He had time for just an instant of doubt. What if the boy didn't get the idea about the tackle box?

"Fuck that."

He started running, following the truck.

A half of a mile down the road he found the first fishing lure.

#

CHAPTER 5

A Back From The Dead Beer Bomb

Running for distance is nothing more than a matter of form and precision. Once you found your form, repetition took over. You fell into a groove if you did it right. As long as you could forget what the road ahead looked like and what the road behind felt like, you could keep on going. You just had to focus on that moment of suspended gravity when your weight was totally supported by momentum and only then did the act of running become sort of easy.

It was harder with the cancer. The doctor had told him that the tumor was too small to feel externally, but right now Hillman felt Big Billy coiling and flexing inside his belly like a ball of wiggling screams filled with barbed wire snakes.

It was harder with the girl, too. His arms were heavy, the biceps swelling and tearing and arguing as he ran. Let her go, his arms said, she's just holding you back.

Hillman kept on running. It had been a lot of years since he'd ran in boots. He couldn't quite remember when or why he'd learned to run like this, but he was glad his body remembered how. Something about the action just felt right, like he'd lost his favorite hat and found it again.

He was just as glad when he saw the fishing lure glinting on the flat black roadway. He was glad because it gave him an excuse to stop running.

He leaned over, lowering the girl's body to the ground. She may have been dead, but he didn't want to drop her.

He nearly fell over himself. His breath was burning in his lungs. Big Billy Tumor was working over his insides like a welterweight working a heavy bag. Hillman felt his heart pounding in his ears. He damn near blacked out. Christ, he couldn't have come so far just to stroke out over a dead girl's body.

"You can't keep this up," the dead woman said.

"You kept up with me just fine."

"Spirits are lighter than flesh. It helps, not having to breathe."

"I can manage," he said.

"You need help, and I can give it."

She reached for the dead girl.

"What are you doing?"

"Ssshh," the dead woman said, pushing a long bony finger into the dead girl's mouth, parting her lips in an almost sexual fashion, the rest of her body liquifying as if she were pouring herself down the dead girl's throat, like some kind of back from the dead beer bomb.

Hillman just stared, not having enough breath for an oh-my-god.

"Now I can run with you," the dead woman said through the dead girl's lips.

"That's wrong," Hillman protested. "You can't be messing with her body like that. That's called desecration."

"Possession is nine-tenths of the law, isn't it? I am dead, she is dead, now we're both dead together. Where's the harm in that?"

Hillman was too tired to argue. He hadn't worked his legs like this in a while. He bent and picked up the lure and forced himself to straighten up.

The lure was a flatfish. His favorite. Mottled green, and easy to spot against the dirt. A rapela, one of the expensive kind, jointed with a half dozen sharpened hooks. He'd caught a hell of a lot of fish with this lure in his time. It was catnip for the bass.

"First catch of the day," he said with a grin.

"Kind of small, don't you think?" a voice sounded directly behind Hillman. "Maybe you ought to throw it back and call it seed?"

Hillman whirled, raising up his shotgun instinctively, his knees folding into a gunfighter's crouch. There, standing in the middle of the road, was the biggest traffic cop Hillman had ever seen. A mountie, all dressed in red with those puffy thighed jodhpurs, that giant Baden Powell boy scout hat, with a face as red as a burning brick shithouse. Not sunburned red, not blood pressure red, not even freckle red. He looked a little native, but it wasn't that kind of red either. It was barn red, like he'd painted it. Like he'd been going to a football game to cheer on his favorite team. Like he'd rinsed his face in a lather of freshly spilled blood.

"Holy Sergeant Pepper Preston," Hillman said. The Mountie was certainly a sight. Dressed like Dudley Do-right and red as a habenero pepper.

Hillman let his breath out slowly, and lowered the shotgun.

"You hunting, or fishing?" the mountie asked.

The mountie was tall, standing at about half past six feet. Dudley Do-right on mega-steroids. He looked to weigh in at a solid two hundred and eighty pounds. A prow of a face, cheeks knotted rock-hard from habitual gum chewing, eyes that looked nearly black. If Hillman fired, he figured the buckshot would just bounce off.

"A little of both," Hillman replied. "I've got my licenses. I've been in a wreck."

The big mountie nodded like he had already heard the story before.

"Deer season ended some time ago," the mountie pointed out.

"I'm hunting small game."

"With a twelve gauge? That's too much gun, unless you're counting on making mince meat."

"Target practice. That's what I'm here for."

"So why do you need a hunting license? You better make up your mind. I'm getting a kind of feeling like maybe you're lying to me. I'm not offended by that. I'm a liar myself. But it bothers me to think that maybe you're planning on shooting someone with that there shotgun."

The mountie was right, of course, but not in the way he figured. Hillman tried to think of a reasonable answer.

"Do you have insurance?" the mountie asked.

Hillman nearly panicked, thinking that the mountie was talking about his life insurance policy.

"I mean on your car. I saw it back there," the mountie said. "It didn't look like it was going anywhere too fast."

Hillman wanted to ask what was with the red paint, but he was afraid the question might delay his pursuit.

"I'm trailing a truck," Hillman explained. Maybe it was just some kind of a sunscreen. Yeah, that's right, sunscreen in October. That made perfect sense.

"On foot?" the mountie asked.

"It's all I've got to work with right now. There's a boy on the truck. He's chained. Maybe kidnapped or something."

The mountie looked down the highway. "Long old road," he said. "Funny how a highway never really ends. It just flows into another road, and on and on it goes."

He turned back to Hillman.

"You figure a kidnapper would cruise around with a kid chained in his truck bed?"

"I've never figured much about kidnappers. I work in a coffeehouse, or at least I used to."

"I know who you are," the mountie said, standing there, popping his gum.

"Everyone keeps telling me that," Hillman said. "But I'll be fucked with a rusty jackhammer if I know what they mean by it."

"Do you got any identification?" the mountie asked.

Hillman fished out his wallet. The mountie took it. Opened it and had a look.

"No pictures? Everybody I know always carries pictures in their wallets. You got no loved ones?"

There was something not real here. Hillman didn't like the look or feel of it.

The mountie adjusted his hat, thumbing the brim to crease it flat.

Hillman was surprised to see the officer dressed this sharply. He looked like a reject from the Musical Ride. Surely he didn't patrol in dress uniform? And what was that red paint about?

"You ought to at least give thanks to *Kji-kinap* for

sending you a fish, even so little a one as that." The mountie gestured towards Hillman's lure. "The spirit don't take too lightly to being shunned."

The lure began to flap in Hillman's hands, like it had been shot full of electricity. The hooks lashed about and its tiny whittled mouth clacked open and closed and the eyes painted across its bright green body rolled in disbelief.

The mountie kept on talking.

"*Kji-kinap.* That's Mi'kmaq for great power. The one who made everything. Spirit. Do you know the story?"

He went on talking, assuming that Hillman would listen.

"It happened a long time ago, back before pay teevee. The great spirit, *Kji-kinap* or *Manitou*, depending on what side of the country you're telling this story, he gets it into his head to make a world out of a ball of crap he'd found on the roadside. He didn't know that the crap belonged to Coyote. He didn't know that the world he was making was in Coyote's image. Now *Kji-kinap* might not remember things that way, but Coyote knows differently."

Hillman was only half listening, busy staring at the lure twisting in his hands. He dropped the lure like it was burning hot. It flapped and struggled in the dirt at his feet.

"Oh now you dropped it. That's no way to treat a fish. Show some respect," the mountie chided.

"It's not a fish," Hillman protested. "It's a fishing lure. It's just wood. It's not alive."

The mountie opened his hand, palm up, and the little lure jumped up like a tiny salmon into the basket of the mountie's splayed fingers. In the instant it took for the lure to land it had grown into a good sized trout.

The mountie held the lure-fish upwards, turning to face all four points of the compass.

"Thank you *Kji-knap* for the gift of this fish, even

though I made it myself."

"Hey I gave it to you," Hillman protested.

"You want it back?" the mountie asked, holding the lure-fish back out towards Hillman's outstretched hands.

Looking closely, Hillman could see a woman's green eyes staring at him from out of the lure's painted surface. Staring hard, like she was trying to tell him something.

He stepped back hastily, nearly running into the dead girl.

"Save the boy," the dead woman said from the dead girl's mouth. She was turned away from him, so that she could look at him from her broken-necked backwards-staring bright green eyes.

The mountie didn't hear or see her. Nobody ever did.

"She with you?" the mountie asked, nodding at the dead girl/woman.

Hillman's eyes widened. No one had ever seen the dead woman before this. Of course, she had never worn a dead girl before this, either.

"Hey little sister," the mountie said. "It has been a long time."

The mountie walked around behind Hillman so that he could look the girl in the face. "Who has used you this way?"

The woman answered in perfect Mi'kmaq, which strangely enough, Hilllman understood.

"He did," the dead woman said, nodding backwards towards Hillman. "But don't hold it against him. He doesn't even remember killing me yet."

Hillman stared blankly. "You see her?" he asked.

"Sure," the mountie said, grinning like Hillman's fly had opened in front of the prime minister. "Don't you?"

"I didn't think anyone else could see her."

"Not everyone has the right kind of eyes," the

mountie said. "I see him, too."

He pointed up the road.

Hillman turned warily. The big bastard's truck was sitting there, just parked over the next rise.

"You see?" the mountie asked. "I see. I have the right kind of eyes. I have the kind of eyes to see anything I can dream. I am Coyote. When a feather falls in the forest the bear may smell it, the rabbit may hear it, the eagle may eye it, but only the Coyote can do all three at once."

"Coyote? Any relation to Wile E, or Peter?" asked Hillman. "I loved you in that last movie of yours. And shouldn't we be doing something about that boy? He's alive, right? I mean, he looks alive to me, but I don't know how long that's going to last."

The mountie reached out to stroke the bark of a tree. The bark stirred beneath his touch like a pillar of suspended oil. "Everything is alive, if you look at it rightly. Even the wood has a spirit. You can hear it singing in the trees in the darkness. It sings to the hunters who have lost their way, and the men who have never come back from the woods. Even the stones have their own tongue, their own life. You can feel it when you hold certain rocks in your hands."

Hillman waved the shotgun threateningly. He didn't know what the fuck was going on, and waving the big gun made him feel he was still a little in control of things.

"Get back," Hillman said. "Or I'll shoot."

The mountie looked at the gun like Hillman had brought it to show and tell.

"Can't you feel the spirit moving in that shotgun? In the wood of the stock? You've tamed it, polished it, sleeked it up with oil and even that has its own song. Are your hands that dead that they can't feel the tune of the wood? The grain running like a stream in your hands?"

A part of Hillman wanted to let the gun go. He was so afraid of feeling it move and twist in his grip.

Everything that had seemed to be so real was slipping from his grasp. He looked around for something a little more real to hang on to, but all he saw was the squad car, maybe a hundred feet back.

It was a big and solid looking Buick. Now that was something he could hang onto, although he couldn't figure out how the car had got there so damned quietly. He hadn't even noticed it there, all that time while he and the mountie had been talking.

"You like that car? I made it myself from a picture in a Canadian Tire catalogue. That's where I made this mountie suit from as well. Props are important in this play called life. They give you something to lean on to."

Hillman was doing his best not to listen, but Coyote kept talking.

"You know what I like best about Canadian Tire? They give you money when you buy stuff from them. What a wonderfully fucked up way to do business. Wal-Mart ought to take notes."

Hillman kept staring at the Buick, concentrating on how undeniably real the big piece of metal was. Then the bumper and the grill of the Buick began to move, like a big fat silver grin, the hood of the car banging up and down. The hood ornament was a dog. Not a bulldog, like on the trucks, but more like Wile E. Coyote. The ornament was galloping, running in space and going nowhere fast.

"Well by fuck, the cancer must have finally got to my brain," Hillman said. "So this is what it's like to go crazy. I hope it doesn't hurt too long."

The dead woman looked over her shoulder, first at Hillman and then back to the Mountie. She tapped her skull significantly.

"You said a mouthful, little sister. White men are all fucked up," the mountie complained. "Like a pair of shoes arguing over who runs the feet. All tongue and laced up too tight, with nothing but stink and fish glue holding them together."

The mountie was smiling now, all teeth and grin like he was getting set to eat Hillman raw. He held the fish lure out ahead of him like an offering.

As he held it out, the shape of the mountie blurred a little, and for a brief instant Hillman saw him wearing a mask and waving a rifle. Hillman nearly squeezed his shotgun's trigger. All he could see was a blur, a dim image, brighter than thought or instinct. A shot of instant reality slapped Hillman right between the eyes.

And then the vision was gone. There was nothing left but the mountie standing there alone, holding out that damned fish lure.

"Don't you even want this fish? It's food, it's good to eat. It's what we're all good at. Eating and fucking and farting. Maybe a little smoke or a dance. All the good things in life. What more do you want?"

Hillman looked back up the road. The big bastard was still stood there, right beside his truck. Just waiting, the red blot of his hunting cap, bright as a burning poppy.

"Is that the truck you're talking about?" the mountie asked.

"That's him," Hillman said.

The mountie popped his chewing gum. There was something loud and irritating in the way in which he popped it, like gunshots going off in a confessional.

"He doesn't seem to be trying that hard to escape," the Mountie said.

"Aren't you going to chase him?" Hillman asked.

The mountie stared, his eyes as hard and flat as polished river stones.

"He's waiting for you," the mountie said. "Maybe you should go and see what he wants."

Then he turned and walked back to his squad car, which had stopped laughing, but was still grinning on the verge of a nasty little snigger.

"Wait," Hillman called out, but the mountie kept on walking. Hillman could have easily have shot him in the back, but what would be the point?

"You know what you've got to do," the mountie said. "Save the boy. Fight the troll. Find the bridge."

"The troll? Is that what that thing in the red hat is?"

The mountie opened the car door. He stepped inside and slammed it closed. He looked out one last time, and yelled, "See if you can find me a beer while you're at it."

Then the mountie drove slowly away, making it a point not to look at his rear view mirror. Hillman wondered how many times had this happened? How many times had the mountie tied a blindfold of excuses around his eyes and glibly looked the other way?

"Coward," Hillman shouted. "You're on his payroll, aren't you?"

Hillman turned and looked back at the truck. The troll had the boy out now, dangling him from his chain like a freshly caught trout. The boy was kicking in midair. The troll held something else up in his other hand. Then he dropped that something else on the ground beside the truck. Hillman didn't need to see anymore to know that the object that the big bastard had dropped was a fishing lure.

Hillman looked back towards the mountie, but the squad car was nowhere in sight. There was nothing there but a big sort of mangy dog, sitting in the middle of the road wagging its shaggy tail, grinning around a fresh caught trout.

"Go find Timmy," Hillman said. "He's in the fucking well."

The truck started to pull away, and Hillman started running after it.

#

CHAPTER 6

The Hill Turned Into A Mountain

There are vectors at work in this universe that can bring two people together from untold dimensions apart. These workings are common in both war and love, and are understood only by the blind gods of chance and circumstance, the accountants of the apocalypse, and certain balloon twisting clowns.

Hillman understood this kind of instant destiny, but running uphill with a loaded shotgun trying to chase a moving truck was just plain stupid. What the fuck was he thinking? He wasn't built for outrunning trucks. He'd left his Flash run-like-lightning boots back home with his Superman up-up-and-away cape and his Casanova jockstrap.

"Save the boy," the dead woman reminded him. At least she wasn't having any problems keeping up.

"You've sure got your line down," Hillman turned to say. Just as he turned he came around a blind corner, and ran smack dab into the side of the truck.

The impact threw him backwards. The truck was hard and the roadside was even harder.

Hillman hit the pavement like a stack of badly flipped flapjacks. Slow motion road rash raked his cheek. He saw a fistful of median-yellow asphalt stars flash bulbing before his eyes. The shotgun wasn't in his hand. It had jumped away like a freshly caught trout.

Hillman looked up and saw the big bastard troll standing over him. Looking down at him with a gaze as hard and sharp as a pair of obsidian arrowheads. Stone eyes, flat and implacable. The windows of this big troll's soul had been painted over in indelible black paint.

The troll grabbed Hillman by his face, yanking him up like a lucky prize out of a crackerjack box. Hillman swung hard, putting a sloppy left cross into the troll's ribs. He might as well have tried to manhandle the pick up truck.

The big troll pounded him against the side of the truck. Hillman did his best to grin, partly to piss the big bastard off and partly to keep his teeth from slamming together and breaking. The troll socked him in the stomach. Hillman wanted to puke. How'd you like that, trollie? A big bellyful of cancerous vomit, with extra diced carrots.

Hillman worked inside, grabbing at the troll's right arm and twisting. He swept a kick against the side of the troll's ankle. It ought to have brought him down, but it didn't. Hillman might have had better luck trying to take down one of those jack pines.

The troll wrapped Hillman's wrist up in a hand the size of a catcher's mitt. He slammed Hillman's knuckles against the truck side. Hillman's arm went numb and tinglish, like it was trying to turn itself into electricity. Another crack like that would likely break bones.

Hillman hooked upwards with his free hand, forking two peace-signed fingers into the big bastard's nostrils. The bastard's boogers felt wet and sticky and somehow alive. Hillman put his hip into the swing, turning the fork into a makeshift uppercut. The troll's face-mask peeled up and off of the big bastard's face.

The troll's real under-the-skin-mask face looked like a fat corduroy watermelon, with eyes like flat oily puddles. There were iridescent colors, insane to describe, running through them like drunken rainbows. His flesh felt as hard as petrified Indian rubber, the mouth double-jointed like that of a snake. His teeth shone out like a fan of razorblades. Hillman figured he had to be careful hitting the big bastard. One wrong jab and he could easily lose a fist.

"Don't blink," Hillman said, as he thumbed the troll

squarely in the middle of his left oily eye puddle. "You've got something in your eye."

The troll twisted and threw Hillman down to the ground. Hillman flapped his hands backwards against the dirt like he was trying to learn how to fly upside down. He caught hold of the shotgun in midflap. He came up kneeling, pointing the shotgun straight at the big bastard, but the boy was in the way. The troll had him dangling by his chain, like a giant kicking and screaming pocket watch.

Damn it. Hillman had nearly forgotten about the boy. How could he do something like that? What kind of a man was he?

"Fine," Hillman said.

He shifted his aim and pumped two blasts into the truck's rear tires. Shifted back to the troll.

"Dangle that kid all you want." He pumped another shell into the chamber. "Now you're afoot too."

The troll threw the chained boy at him. Hillman tried to catch him and keep hold of the shotgun at the same time. It was a stupid plan. The boy fell, and Hillman stumbled reaching out for him and the shotgun hit the ground again.

Hillman tried to regain his footing. The troll was a wall in front of him, a wall that grew a door that slammed Hillman down and back and off of the side of the road.

Too bad they were parked beside a hill.

Hillman toppled down the hill, tumbling like a one-man avalanche, cartwheeling like a drunken Soviet gymnast, completely out of control.

The hill grew into a mountain halfway down and Hillman blacked out halfway past that.

#

CHAPTER 7
Thoughts On The Other Side of The Mask

Stupid, the troll thought to himself.

He should have seen that coming. The little man, shooting out his tires like that. Why hadn't he seen it happening?

He was thinking like a stone. He didn't want to go back there into the ground, not yet. Old one-eye would have laughed his hole off had he seen it happen.

That damned coyote. It was his fault.

Who was this man? The troll had hunted so many before this. Why did this one seem so different?

He remembered the Norsemen hunting him with torches and long iron spears. They hadn't bested him, until the gods took a hand. Old one-eye and that silver-tongued trickster.

Killing him and putting him in the rock. Thinking he'd stay.

The problem with the Norsemen was that they spent too much time thinking about death. Their Ragnarok, they ran from it like a rabbit from the wolves.

Stupid men. When death comes you cannot run from it.

The Mi'kmaq hunters had known that. Even the settlers who'd tried to track him knew how close to death a man truly lives. All of fate, everything that is a man's destiny wears a chain that is forged link by link by the hammer blows of blind fate. Control is nothing but an illusion.

Urd, Verdandi and Skuld spun their threads and no man could say when the sickle would fall just as sure as the bridge swung high in the heavens.

He had escaped into the stone, swum through the

long cool silent darkness, until he had finally emerged here in the land across the gray waters where Odin had woven his secret bridge. Now he must stay and guard it. That had been the pact. That had been the contract.

"Can we go home now?" the boy asked. "We don't need her."

The troll eyed the boy.

"Not the way you let her loose, do we?"

He dragged the boy close to him. He'd found him on the roadside, with his parents. He had pushed the car into a lake and fed the fishes with his parents' bones. He kept the father's face and made this mask from it.

Stone it. He'd nearly lost everything.

Why hadn't he seen that coming?

"You're hurting me," the boy said.

The troll felt the warmth of the boy's skin, his heart beating like a softly muffled drum, as steady as the tide. He knew what to do.

"Come here boy," he said, reaching for the boy. Reaching deep into the boy's chest.

#

CHAPTER 8

Besides, Bob Hope's Dead

Bob Hope had it all wrong. Memory wasn't anything to be thankful for.

Memory was a kissing cousin to guilt, twice removed.

Memory was a dark country road you don't always want to travel down, even when you have to.

Memory was the mildew of the soul. Wash as often as you wish and all the old stains kept bleeding through.

Hillman rolled back into unconscious oblivion,

following the stream of his thought on a one-way trip down a dark memory lane.

He could see himself standing behind the counter, waiting for a customer to choose between a cappuccino and a café latte.

Then the kid came in the doorway. He was wearing a hockey mask with a rubber machete jammed through it. He reminded Hillman of Steve Martin, with his old arrow-in-the-head gag.

"This is a stick-up!" the kid shouted, a product of too many gangster movies.

Hillman turned towards the kid. All of a sudden Hillman looked like Gary Cooper, standing there with a six-gun strapped to a side, his badge lying in the dirt beside a dead Quaker woman's body.

"Draw," the kid said, waving a rifle with more barrels than a Milwaukee brewery.

"How lucky do you feel, pilgrim?" Hillman drawled.

Just then the woman walked into the store. Hillman heard the bells ringing merrily. Was it Christmas already? Strange time to hold it, in the middle of July.

Hillman reached for his pistol. The kid, half turning towards the woman, squeezed a shot off from his multi-barreled mega-blaster, each of the barrels metamorphosing into a screaming open mouth.

Hillman felt the shot hitting him like a soft wet hammer, tearing through the meat of his left shoulder. He felt Big Billy bouncing pain through his nervous system like a runaway pinball.

The kid raised his hockey mask, and underneath it was the troll, black and hard and chitinous, with a pair of shiny steel sheriff's badges for eyes.

"Badges," the troll snarled. "We don't need no stinking badges."

Hillman pushed past the pain, forcing his pistol up into a firing position. The kid had his uber-rifle trained on the woman. She was standing there screaming, like she'd stepped into a burning building. The kid screamed with her, spittle spraying around him. Hillman opened his mouth to scream a three-part harmony, but because he'd been holding his breath a mouthful of spittle slathered down his chin. It felt wet, like blood.

Hillman squeezed the trigger.

A pair of long silver scissors sheared through a knotted cord upon the counter, a chain of circumstances breaking at a certain critical link.

I have to remember this, Hillman thought. I have to remember what this all means.

The woman screamed louder and the last thing that Hillman remembered was staring at the unblinking emerald compass of her large bright green eyes as one of them shattered out.

#

CHAPTER 9

Where's Marcus Welby When You Really Need Him?

Hillman roused from his dreams, alarm-clocked awake by the squawk of a screaming blue jay. It sounded like the bird didn't much like him being here. Hillman kind of shared the feeling.

He was lying on his back. His arms and legs felt to be in the right places and at the right angles, but he was a little afraid of moving them.

"Hold still," the dead woman said.

Hillman looked down. She was putting something on his wounded leg.

"What's that?" he asked.

"You don't want to know."

"It's funny, I thought I just asked."

"Powdered puffballs and cobwebs. I'd chew some ash bark for you, to take the swelling down, but I couldn't see any around. The puffballs and webbing will help clot your bleeding. Try chewing this willow bark for the pain."

"Great. I'm getting medical aid from Ewell Gibbons. Where's Marcus Welby when you really need him?" He let her continue. He wasn't crazy about what she was doing, but it did seem to help halt the bleeding.

He looked up at the trees laughing down at him. Standing there, thrust upward like tall raw bones, bowing and not bowing, their roots clawing and worming into the dirt. Healthy, not rotten like he was. They belonged here. They fit.

Hillman sure didn't belong out here. What had he been thinking about, taking on that big bastard like that? He could have been killed.

"Wasn't that the whole point?" the dead woman asked.

"This is a hell of a time to start growing a sense of humor," Hillman said, with a laugh. Once he had laughed, once he had broken the tension that held him fast, he could find the strength to move.

He sat up and looked at the dead woman. He was glad to have her along, even if she was nothing more than a guilty hallucination. She was company.

"I like you too," said the dead woman.

"Oh you can read minds now."

She smiled. "I can do whatever you want me to. I'm your fantasy, not mine."

"Do you have a name, or should I dream you up one?"

"Call me Lily. It's what my grandmother used to call me."

"Is that your name, or the little girl's?"

"I'm not sure," she said.

He clambered up the hill, feeling his legs moving beneath his denim jeans.

"You're walking slower," she said. "Do you want me to find something for that?"

"Are you going to wrap me in seaweed and slime mold? To hell with that. If you can find me a case of beer and a steak, that'll fix me up just fine. Besides, I'm just limping for sympathy."

"Is that you want? For me to feel sorry for you? You're the one who killed me."

"I don't remember that."

"You will," she said. "Just think about it."

He tried his hardest to think. He knew that Lily was somehow connected with his memories of the coffee shop. He just couldn't remember how. He couldn't remember much at all about the coffee shop. He ran it. He served coffee.

He remembered the kid walking in and waving the rifle.

He reached the top of the hill and his recollections still played hide and seek in the graveyard of his memories. Like a little boy, running through the shadows – can't find me, can't find me.

He pulled himself up to the road.

The truck was demolished. The cab beat down, the doors pulled off, the engine knocked clean off of its block. It looked like the big bastard had taken out his frustration on the Ford.

"Good," Hillman said. He'd pissed the troll off. That was really good. The angrier the big bastard got, the stupider he'd behave. That was good to know. He hadn't liked Hillman shooting out his tires. He hadn't expected it.

That was good to know too. Whatever the big bastard was, it wasn't all that smart. It wasn't infallible.

He stared at the dents in the truck's side. It looked like the troll had taken a sledge hammer to it. Shit. The big bastard was strong.

"Well you knew that all ready, didn't you?" he said aloud. He was beginning to get used to talking to himself. That was either a good sign or a bad one.

He took a quick stock of his arsenal. He had a Zippo lighter and a four inch buck knife. He supposed he could make a garotte out of his belt, except that it was currently holding his pants up. He didn't want to charge into battle in his boxers.

He had nothing but the bare necessities. Baloo and Tarzan would have both approved.

He rooted through the wreckage. He found a styrofoam cooler, and a bottle of Knob Creek bourbon. One hundred proof. If he didn't manage to shoot the big bastard, he could always stand around and wait for its liver to fail.

He unscrewed the cap and took a swallow. It burned going down, a blast of fire and grain and madness. Hillman felt the blood rushing to his head, his face burning. The drink was stronger than he liked, but fuck it. If the big bastard could drink this shit, Hillman wasn't going to wuss out now.

"I'M DRINKING YOUR LIQUOR, YOU UGLY TWO-FACED BASTARD!" Hillman yelled at the top of his lungs. Yelling was hard work, given the strength of the bourbon. He took another swallow. Choked, and found his breath.

"It's good, too," he croaked.

"You should be careful," Lily warned him. "Too much of that will cloud your reason. You'll want to have your wits about you when you face him."

He grinned at her.

"Don't approve of me mingling with other spirits?" He took another swallow.

A part of him wanted to empty the bottle, but he forced himself to pour it out. He cut some hosing from the engine, and used it to siphon some gas from the tank into the empty bottle. Then he broke up the styrofoam and pushed it into the bottle. When he was finished constructing his homemade bomb he rescrewed the cap back onto the bottle. He'd stuff a rag in it when he got close enough to fling it at the troll. Until then, he didn't trust just leaving it open. The gasoline might evaporate, or worse yet soak his rucksack.

"Stick a rag in there, light it and chuck it. Be a hot old time, you bet."

"You figure that'll hurt him?" Lily asked.

"I figure it'll prove enlightening." He looked at her. She seemed to know so much. "Do you have any better ideas?"

She didn't answer.

He tucked the makeshift molotov into his rucksack. As he was straightening up he noticed the message.

"Isn't that sweet," Hillman said. "He left me a note."

The message was gouged into the side of a granite cut-off.

Lord, how strong could that big bastard be?

The message he'd carved was simple. IF YOU WANT THE BOY, COME AND GET HIM: Hillman read it aloud.

"Makes it sound easy, doesn't he?"

Hillman turned around. The big mountie was back, standing there like he'd never left. His face was still painted red. He looked more native than ever. The squad car squatted just a little ways down the road, sniggering quietly.

"He's fishing for you. You know that, don't you? Like one of those angler fish, deep in the ocean, dangling a bit of glowing meat, you grab it and then there's nothing but teeth."

"Don't you have any sort of protecting and serving to do?" Hillman asked.

“I know what I’ve got to do,” the mountie said. “Can you say the same?”

“It beats the fuck out of me what you figure I’ve got to do. I’ve got a life you know?”

“Yeah? And what you were getting set to do with that life when you got out here?”

“Is that was this is about? Are you some kind of guardian angel, come to keep me from killing myself?”

The mountie laughed.

“I ain’t no angel, that’s for sure. And what makes you think I’m here for you?”

“Well then who the hell are you? I know you’re not any kind of mountie I’ve ever seen. And who’s that troll I’ve been chasing?”

“Slow down, white man. You’re chasing too many rabbits. You chase one rabbit, you got yourself a supper. You chase too many, and all you got is sad sore feet. Didn’t your father teach you anything? I told you, I’m Coyote. I taught the rainbow how to sing, and birds how to whisper.”

“Birds don’t whisper.”

“They do in the night time, when you’re too asleep to listen. It’s a story, that’s all. I am the story and I am the teller. You’re just another set of ears, so listen.”

The mountie picked up a rock.

“Stories live forever. They’re just like stones. Stones are the bones of the earth. Everything else rots while stone endures. There is a long vein of stone. Serpentine, you white men call it. It crawls from the northlands of Russia, through the Scandinavian fjords and the British Isles right down under the Atlantic to the Maritimes and down into the Appalachians. The old Norsemen called it The Great Serpent. They swore it went right around the world. What the fuck did those frost-balled snow-worshipping seadogs know of the world? They turned tail at the first signs of arrowheads and blood. Paddled themselves all the way back home."

The mountie laughed at the conjuring of that memory.

"That's when he came over. Old Daddy Redcap. He's a troll. He came through the stone, following the scent of the norsemen. When he got here they were all gone. Fucking vikings. They wore horns on their hats so as they'd have somewhere to hang their hats on."

"That's a myth," Hillman said.

"Huh?"

"The horned helmets. Hollywood thought them up because they figured they looked cool. Vikings didn't really wear helmets like that. You've been misinformed. Perhaps you ought to stop reading so much Hagar The Horrible."

The mountie looked at Hillman in disbelief.

"Are you calling me a liar?" He leaned forward like a one hundred foot lodgepole pine, getting set to fall.

"You loom really well," Hillman said. "Am I supposed to be frightened?"

The mountie cracked a smile. Then he laughed out loud.

"Ha! You might be right. I don't mind. I am a liar. I always have been. Don't trust a damn thing that comes out of my mouth. Coyote the liar, Coyote the thief."

"That's good to know," Hillman said.

"I'm a myth, too," said the mountie. "Just like the dinosaurs."

Hillman was having fun with this.

"Dinosaurs aren't myths."

"Sure they are. Great big giant thunder lizards? Mesozoic, protozoic, fuckyouzoic, none of that horseshit ever happened.

"What about fossils?"

"Just dragon and giant bones. Scientists dreamed up all of that hooraw about dinosaurs and the like just to keep the whole world grounded in the superstitions of reality. They had to. It wouldn't do to have folks believing in mythology, going on all pagan and such like. Next thing you know they'd stop going to church and paying taxes. The whole civilized world would grind to a halt."

"But there *were* dinosaurs."

"Oh for a little while. One of them, anyway. A big old lizard. A meat eater. He used to chase the natives around in the night time. I tracked him to his lair. Figured out he was allergic to sunshine. So I shot an arrow into the sun, and then I shot a second arrow into the butt end of the first arrow."

"I thought that was Robin Hood."

"Are you telling this story or me?"

Hillman held his hands up in acquiescence. Coyote went on talking.

"Once I'd shot enough arrows I dragged the sun down and tucked it in a mud pond. Then the lizard came out of his cave, thinking it was dark. Once he was far enough away from his cave, I set the sun free. He turned blind in that sudden bright light. I taunted him into running into a tar pit, and that's how Coyote invented fossils."

"That's not much of a story."

"It's not a story. It's the truth."

"Right. Okay. So what's our plan?"

"Why ask me?" the large cop asked. "You're the one who is supposed to know what he's got to do."

"Do you want me to sing Oh Canada, or just patriotically whistle while you go mount yourself?" Hillman asked. "You know more than I do. Tell me what to do."

"Hold out your hand," the mountie said.

Hillman did so. The mountie dropped something into his hand.

A police badge.

"That's a myth too, until you start remembering it."

"Are you deputizing me?"

"Save the boy," the mountie said.

Hillman looked at the badge. There was something about it that was damned familiar, even though it was made to look like a plastic sheriff's badge.

"Is this for real?"

"It's as real as you want to believe."

Hillman tucked the badge into his many pocketed vest. He turned away, looking down the road. When he turned back the mountie was gone. The dog had returned looking a little scruffier. Only it wasn't a dog. Hillman could see that now.

It was a coyote.

Hillman shook his head, ignoring the coyote. He was ready to hunt but which way should he go? Odds are, the big bastard would stay to the road, but he didn't have to. Now that he was on foot, the options increased dramatically.

He stared at the road, searching for any sign of tracks.

There was nothing. He'd lost the trail.

Then he spotted a lure in the center of the road. A red wriggler, with colors that sundowned through the shades of red and orange and yellow. An antique, one left to him by his grandfather.

What should he do with it?

All he could think of was an old trick he remembered his grandmother teaching him, for finding things that had been lost. He'd seen her do it time and again with misplaced thimbles and missing spoons.

He unpocketed his lure. He hefted it in his right hand, still tender from the big bastard's squeeze. He spun around three times repeating: "St. Anthony, St. Anthony, look around. There's something lost that must be found."

On the third turn he threw the red wriggler over his

right shoulder, then whirled about quickly to see where it landed.

He spotted the wriggler as it landed. He stepped over to it.

"Well, say son of a bitch and five hail Mary's on the fifty yard line, St. Anthony did the trick!"

The lure was lying directly beside a second lure. It was a lipstick shiny blood red Winchester minnow.

The big bastard was still leaving a bread crumb trail.

"Obliging of him," Hillman said.

The coyote barked behind him. Hillman turned. The damned thing was sitting up.

"You want this?" he asked.

"You're damned right," the coyote said.

The coyote was talking, just like before. Hillman hadn't imagined it. He couldn't believe what he was seeing. He had seen a fishing lure transformed into a live fish, and was stalking a troll but he drew the line at talking dogs.

"I'm no dog. I am Coyote. Sometimes I walk on two legs, sometimes I walk on four, sometimes I walk on eight and sometimes I don't use any at all."

"I don't believe in myths," Hillman said.

"You probably don't really believe in St. Anthony either, but he worked for you didn't he?" The Coyote wagged his tail. "St. Anthony. Now that was an interesting guy. He followed St. Francis, in that he loved to talk to fish. He petted me once in a graveyard outside of Sicily. A good man. He knew how to scritch behind the ears. Really quiet too. He kept his mouth shut for the early part of his priesthood, until somebody asked him to speak in public at the age of 23 and he never learned to shut up again. Hold something down for too long a time and it's all going to come back up."

Hillman thought about that. Coyote kept on talking.

"St. Anthony was a good man and the only Catholic

Saint to be recognized by the North American Indians. That's the truth, or at least that's what people tell. Myth, truth, there's no difference. Myths are just misplaced memories. Lies told sweetly, thoughts gathered into a story-like shape."

Hillman dropped the lure. The coyote ran in and snapped it up.

"Give me the other one," he said.

"I need it to find the next lure."

"You don't need St. Anthony any more. You've got me. Throw that damned lure."

Hillman threw the lure up into the air. The coyote caught it before it hit the ground, neatly avoiding the hooks.

"Follow me," The coyote said. "I've got the taste and the scent. Come on. He went this way."

Hillman started down the path, following the coyote and the trail of lures, wondering whether he was fishing or being fished for.

The dead woman followed close behind. The coyote stayed a constant wary two steps behind her.

"I love a parade," the coyote said, his tongue lolling happily from the side of his open mouth like a long red wet battle-flag.

#

CHAPTER 10

Fishing In Shadows

"Here's another one," Hillman called out. He bent and picked the lure up. A flasher, all small and thin and jointed and silver.

Hillman looked back at the coyote. "You want to eat this one too?"

He threw the lure into the air without waiting for an answer. As it reached the apogee of its arc the coyote transformed it into another fish. He caught it in midair and snapped it down.

Lily watched the coyote eat without saying anything. She'd been strangely quiet since the coyote had joined the hunt. Hillman didn't think she approved of the coyote's company.

"You ever think to magic me up a hamburger while you're busy finding Nemo?" Hillman asked.

The coyote grinned. Hillman had seen dogs grin before, but there was something a little sly about the coyote's smile, as if the coyote were imagining a secret joke that involved a nude Hillman with a barrel of long spined cactus.

"Why didn't you bring some food of your own?" Coyote asked. "Try some of those pigeon berries."

"I had jerky. You stole it."

"I think you misplaced it," Coyote retorted.

Hillman gave it up as a lost argument.

"Look, we've been hunting for three hours. It's nearly dark and I'm hungry." He knelt and grabbed a handful of the hard white pigeon berries, nibbling them dutifully. They were chalky and raw tasting. He worked them down, swallowing hard at the last of it. They were barely edible.

"Can you eat these things?" Hillman asked.

Big Billy Bellytumor sure didn't care for the pigeon berries. He sent cramps, and a thin squirt of diarrhea. Hillman grunted his discomfort and kept on walking. When cancer crawled into your inner workings, dignity died an early death.

"You can eat a lot of things," Coyote assured him. "But I like fish. Hurry, and let's find another."

"I'm hungry," Hillman repeated.

"What about that tin of beans you've got in your

sack? Why don't you open those? Scoop them out cold."

Hillman looked away. "I'm saving them," he said, not meeting Coyote's gaze.

"Ha!" Lily laughed. "You forgot to bring your can opener, didn't you?"

"It might be a long hunt, and I'm saving them," Hillman repeated.

"Ha. Some woodsman. Mark Trail would laugh his Bob Dobb's pipe right out of his mouth. You should learn to fish. Didn't you ever learn?"

"I left the rod in the Volvo. I know how to fish. My dad taught me."

"Right. Father and son camporee, I bet you. Saturday night, once a year. Am I getting close?"

Hillman scowled. "My father was a railroad man. He loved to fish. We went once a month, down to the river."

Hillman thought of his father. A dark and distant man who stank of diesel and iron. A man who lived on a mountain in the middle of his home, always so distant and unapproachable. He worked night shifts and slept on the couch in the daytime. The living room was heavy with the stink of night breath and snoring, like a chainsaw drowning in tar-oil. Everyone lived on tiptoe, for fear of waking the ogre.

"What are you thinking about?" Coyote asked.

"When we fished together. It was our best times. It was kind of like a treaty we made with each other. The only kind of time that me and my father could speak the same language."

Hillman remembered the river, and the quick little trout, the fat lazy bass, the angry sharp-nosed pike, and the inedible nuisance perch. There was no telling what you'd pull up from those dark waters. Once he'd caught a great ugly eel. He'd wanted to throw it back but his father said a man ought to eat what he caught. He fried it up and forced Hillman to eat a bite. Afterwards, Hillman puked and it tasted like sogged out regret.

Hillman swallowed. His mouth was dry. Damn it. Why hadn't he thought to bring water? He hadn't even packed a canteen in the car. Why should he? He'd never planned on travelling this far into the woods. He'd told himself that if he got thirsty before he killed himself he could always stop at a gas station and pump a few quarters into a soda pop machine. Or maybe a tavern. Yes, that would be a plan.

Hillman tried not to think about beer. It would only make him crazy. He tried not to think about the Knob Creek he'd poured out on to the ground. He imagined it taking root and sprouting a shiny bottle tree ripe with bottles of finely aged bourbon. Why not? He was talking to a dog. How much crazier could today get?

"Coyote, not dog," Coyote corrected.

The molotov sloshed thickly in Hillman's rucksack. A part of Hillman wondered what the gasoline and styrofoam would taste like on his tongue. He wondered if maybe the coyote could work some sort of water to wine magic for him. Turn gasoline to beer?

He told himself to stop that kind of thinking. He hadn't gone that long without water. In the morning he could lick the dew from the leaves.

He almost laughed at how good that plan felt. If only he'd thought of bringing along a plastic bag of some sort, so that he could rig up a catch basin.

Stupid. Plans are dreams made practical.

"Stop dreaming," he told himself.

Night was falling like the lid of a coffin. The deeper they climbed into the mountainous woods, the darker it turned. The shadows breathed from the rocks, bushes rattled ominously, a rabbit ran past Hillman and he damn near had a heart attack.

Coyote nearly choked himself laughing, rolling backwards and kicking his legs in the air.

Hillman waited until he felt he'd recovered enough of his dignity.

"It's getting dark," he said. "We ought to make some kind of a camp, before it gets too dark to see."

Nobody disagreed.

Hillman bow-bent a pine sapling down, and rigged a lashing with his belt to hold it taut against another tree. He hacked and broke what branches he could to make himself a lean-to. He scuffed a clear area with his boots, and then dug out a small fire pit. Finally he gathered kindling in the dark, scraping bark from the pale ghost birches.

He had a fire, and a place to sleep. It had taken nearly an hour and a half. He still wasn't certain who he really was, but he knew one thing for certain. He was no woodsman.

"You don't make coffee, either," Coyote said.

"Are you going to tell me something or keep dropping hints like turds?"

In answer, Coyote raised his tail and dropped a load of rancid feces.

Hillman wrinkled his nose. He crouched, staring up at the stars. Then, when they began to look like eyes looking down, he watched the fire.

A screech owl screamed out a warning in the darkness. Hillman damned near shit his pants. Careful, he told himself. It's not like he could just pick up a spare pair of trousers. He wouldn't want the big bastard to smell him coming.

The scare was good for him. It woke him up long enough to realize he'd been blinding himself by staring too hard at the fire. He forced himself to look into the darkness, just beyond the flames.

That big bastard was out there somewhere. Pissed off at the little store clerk who'd given him such grief.

He could see Coyote out there, just at the edge of the fire, flicking his tail back and forth over his shoulder, making it stretch impossibly long and then casting it out.

"What are you up to now?" Hillman asked.

"Fishing," Coyote said. "I'm hungry."

"Where's the river?"

"All around us," Coyote said. "Time's a river. Memories are just shoals that tie the currents into tidy little forget-me-knots. Myths are strings tied around the fingers of the gods, to help us remember."

"What in the hell are you talking about?"

"Shh. Watch closely and learn, white man."

He cast his tail out, hunkering down and arcing it over his back, sending it impossibly far out into the night shadows.

"This tail is a damn useful contraption. I used it to steal fire once, stuck it in the campfire of the gods and run for earth, trailing little comets behind me. I didn't think it'd ever grow back, but it come back in just like jackpines following a forest fire."

He wiggled his butt, making his balls swing like windblown coconuts.

"I used to have a beautiful coat. Gambled with the beaver and lost, damn them. Right in the middle of winter. I damned near froze until a tribe of field mice took pity on me and gave me their leftover scraps of fur to cobble together this ragbag of a pelt. It's all I've got, but it's warm in the winter and cold in the summer."

He kept twisting his haunches up and back and working his tail like he was trying to hook something.

"This is trickier than it looks," Coyote said. "Easy…easy…ha! Got one."

He yanked his tail back. There was something hanging onto it, like a ball of ill-made shadows. Coyote shook it off the end of his tail, landing it somewhere close to the flames.

"There you go. I've hooked in a shadow and brought us some help," Coyote said. "I figured a few reinforcements never hurt."

The shadow straightened out itself, unkinked its back, and knelt close to the flames. Hillman could see it clearly now. It was a hunter in dirty buckskin, tainted with the reek of old animal fat and honest sweat. He held a long lethal-looking musket, with a crude leather strap wound once about his arm for safekeeping. There was a powder horn on his hip, and a bag of lead shot. He looked a little like the big mountie.

"I don't need any help," Hillman asserted.

"Ha," Lily laughed. "Listen to the one-man army. You're crippled, and that troll damned near took your head off the last time you tangled with him."

Hillman patted his shotgun. "I'll be ready this time."

"You need help," Lily repeated. "Besides, he only brought the one of them. I'm sure a single ghost won't cramp your style that much."

"Two, counting you," Hillman said.

"Three!" Coyote called out, casting in another shadow.

This one was cruder, like a mismade clay sculpture of a man, with a long wooden spear, a knife and a short club swinging at his belt. A necklace of teeth and claws dangling from his wired neck. His shoulders were corded, like a hawk's.

"That's the savage," the hunter said. "At least that's what we call him. He don't talk much, but he's damn useful in a scrap."

The hunter banged out his pipe, shaking out a sprinkle of tiny ghost ashes into the campfire, and kept on talking.

"He got that scar on his leg from a scrap with a cave bear," the hunter said. "The same bear whose teeth and claws are hanging from that necklace around his throat. Like I said, a good man in a scrap."

The savage began drumming the butt of his spear

softly in the dirt. As if on cue, Lily stood up and began to dance by the light of the campfire. She was graceful, for a dead woman.

She sang a song in words that sounded vaguely native. Hillman couldn't recognize the words or the language, but a part of him wanted to stand up and dance with her. It was a little like the feeling he used to get in high school, standing on one side of the gymnasium, trying to muster the courage to cross over that no-man's stretch of hardwood flooring into the girl's side to ask someone if they would care to dance.

Lily turned and looked at him. It felt as if she were looking through the hole in her skull, like she could see through all of the eyes of the maggots that crawled within. Hillman could still see them, just behind the little girl's eyes, like a photograph developing on top of another.

Hillman thought that she'd been kind of pretty, before the bullet had done its work. Not for the first time he wondered how she had come to be that way, and why she was haunting him.

"Who shot you?" he asked.

"A cave bear," she said, with a grin that was almost girlish. "In a travelling circus. He was supposed to be tame, but he wasn't."

"That's a funny joke, but I don't recollect you mentioning an answer. So who shot you?"

"You know who," Lily said. "Or you will."

Hillman wondered if she was flirting with him. He'd never flirted with a dead woman before. It seemed a little pre-necrophiliac to him. What the hell. Maybe being seriously suicidal brought you a little closer to being able to accept the darkness.

"You are growing a sense of humor, aren't you?" Hillman said.

She shrugged. He could see her bones moving beneath her skin, like buried ivory. "I'm closer to my world, out here. I never was a city girl. These woods make me feel at home. I wish I could be buried out here."

"You need a cemetery, don't you?"

She shrugged. "It doesn't matter to us. Anywhere a Mi'kmaq is buried is sacred ground. That's a rule, you know?"

"So where is your body?"

"You know where they put it. You killed me, after all."

Hillman shook his head with real regret. "I don't remember."

"It wasn't your fault, but you felt it was."

"I still don't remember. I don't think I can."

"You will," she said. "And then you will know what you have to do."

"I know all ready. I have to save the child. You've told me. But what is it that I'm saving the child from?"

She paused, as if she were listening to a voice on the wind.

"That isn't all you have to do, but you will know that too when the time comes. A hard wind will blow the smoke from your eyes."

"My doctor told me to cut down," he said with a grin. "Risk of cancer, you know."

"There, see, you can grow a sense of humor too."

She looked away again. Listening. She was definitely listening. Hillman wished he knew what she was listening to.

"Maybe we're just getting to like each other," Hillman suggested.

She shook her head with a laugh. "Forget it. You're not my type. Too white and too alive. Besides, I'm too young now."

"Too white? Isn't that a little like bigotry?"

She laughed. "Not at all. I have had white men before, but you are way too white. Don't you ever tan?"

"Blame it on an over dependency on sunscreen. Maybe I should take some tanning lessons from your red faced friend."

He nodded at Coyote.

Lily's face darkened. Hillman couldn't tell if she was blushing or angry.

"He isn't my friend," she said. "He isn't anybody's friend. But he might help us, if he wants to. We call him *Kluskap*, but that really isn't his name. In some worlds they call him trickster, joker, coyote, raven, anansi. He wears a lot of masks. I don't know what's underneath them all. I don't even know if he remembers. He does what he will, when he wants to, but I think he might help us."

"Why?"

"Because Coyote doesn't like the troll. In another world, where Coyote was called Loki, he and the troll had a long argument."

"How do you know all these things?"

She fixed him once more with that maggot eye microscope moving behind her little girl eyes.

"How do you know when to be afraid of the dark?" she asked.

"I'm not afraid."

"You have been. As a child, when you were closer to the old knowledge, and in lives before that. You just have to forget about not knowing, and then you will remember."

"This isn't a Hare Krishna thing, is it? Will I need to meditate, or get in touch with my inner child, or maybe tie my legs into pretzel knots before I understand what the hell you're talking about?"

"No. This isn't religious, or philosophical, or any other form of wishful thinking. This is for real."

He knew she was lying about something, but he didn't see any reason to contradict her.

"It sounds like a fairy tale," h said.

"A lot of people tell it that way. Like a legend. Like a folk tale. It makes it easier for them to sleep at night."

"So how can this troll be killed?"

She shrugged again.

"I see," Hillman said. "How would you know? You're just a phantom of my guilt."

"I can tell you one thing," she said. "I can tell you where he came from."

She pointed out into the darkness. "He came from out there."

Hillman looked out into the dark night. For a moment the moon looked just like a fish hook, and the stars resembled the shimmered glitter of shoal water. Shapes swam in the darkness between the stars.

Hillman shivered without meaning to.

"And there were giants in the earth," Coyote softly called. "One's closer than you'd like."

Further out into the shadows, just for a half an instant Hillman thought he saw a bridge arcing out into the shadowed darkness like a long dark rainbow.

And just then, something plunged straight into the camp.

#

CHAPTER 11

And Bambi Wept

Hillman sat up in his shelter, startled by the sudden intrusion of the dark shape.

Shit. All this work setting up camp. What had he been thinking? He should have made himself a weapon instead. A spear, or a club, or anything.

Hillman slid his buck knife out, snapping it open in

mid-motion. At the same time he grabbed a chunk of firewood from the woodpile he'd gathered. It was rotted, but better than nothing. If the big bastard wanted to take him, Hillman was determined to go down fighting.

Only the intruder wasn't moving. Just lying there, a shape swallowed by shadows. The savage was squatting up beside it. Whatever the intruder was, the savage looked like he was trying to eat it.

"I think it's supper," the hunter said.

"Did you call out for a pizza?" Lily asked.

Hillman crept closer. In the flicker of the dying firelight, the shape looked like some great beast, waiting to pounce.

Wait or move?

Hillman decided. He crept closer, his knife out and ready, close to his hip where he could swing and cut without risking someone grabbing his blade.

The savage knelt beside whatever it was, tearing it raw with his teeth. It was a dead deer. It looked as if its head had been torn off. Hillman stepped closer.

"I guess the troll doesn't want us to starve," he said.

"Maybe he's just fattening us up for the kill?" Lily suggested.

"Cheery thought."

Coyote thought it was the funniest thing he'd ever seen.

"I thought jumping at the rabbit was bad, but hiding from a dead deer. Deer god, Bambi would piss his little white tail laughing."

"Is this your doing?" Hillman asked, ignoring the remark. "Or is this manna from heaven?"

Coyote shook his head. "Not me white man, nor the old cross guy either."

Hillman shrugged. There was no sense in looking a gift horse in the mouth. Weren't those the last words of the Trojans, right before they dragged in that fat wooden horse? Or was that "Beware of gifts, bearing Greeks?"

Hillman peered into the shadows noosed about the campfire's perimeter. No sign of the big bastard.

Hillman wondered if the meat was poisoned. He snorted at his foolish caution. He had to face facts. If the troll wanted him dead, it just had to walk into the camp while Hillman was sleeping and rip his head off. The big bastard could probably do it with one hand barb-wired behind his back.

Hillman sliced some strips of meat from the carcass. He laid a few against the rocks of his campfire to slow roast.

Hunter did the same.

"I didn't think ghosts ate," Hillman said.

Hunter grinned a soft and dangerous smile. "I'm not exactly a ghost."

"A spirit then. Do you still need to eat?"

"Hunger's one of the last things to die off."

Hillman tore into another strip of meat. He might shit and puke this before morning, but he'd enjoy it for now.

Hillman looked out into the woods, a wild grin dancing on his face as he yelled into the darkness. "I don't suppose you could hunt me up a couple of dozen cold beer while you're at it?"

No answer. He hadn't really expected one.

He roasted the meat, gnawing on it long before the meat had cooked through. Deer meat was healthy, wasn't it? Less cholesterol, more protein. Bambi was never sick a day in his life.

Hunter lay down a little ways from the fire.

Lily stood up from the child's body and it dropped behind her like a small felled tree. Her spirit-form stepped away.

"You ought to be more careful with that body," Hillman said.

"She's honest dead," Lily said. "She doesn't feel a thing. Besides, it feels good to get up and stretch."

She walked over to the hunter and sat down beside him. He smiled and she touched his cheek.

Well what do you know, Hillman thought. He guessed hunger wasn't the only thing that didn't die in spirits.

The two of them, the hunter and Lily, embraced in the shadows. The night seemed to move and sigh around them. There didn't seem to be any real penetration. Just a gentle blending, like shadows coming together. There was a sound, soft and wet and wistful, in the way of death making life. Hillman could hear it over the night breeze. It seemed almost peaceful like the moon over a graveyard.

"Nothing like a little honest friction," Coyote said, licking his lips.

The savage didn't want any part of their monkey business. He crouched out in the furthest ring of the campfire, tearing at his share of the meat, his muscles taut and tensed like a hound ready to pounce.

Coyote lay as close to the fire as he could, leisurely gnawing on his portion. Hillman would have sworn that the Coyote had half an eye on what the Hunter and Lily were up to.

"Damned reprobate," Hillman muttered ruefully, but if the Coyote heard he gave no sign. "Take a picture, it'll last you longer."

"There is no photograph with as strong a cord as memory, or did you forget?" the Coyote said.

Hillman didn't answer. He reached for the girl's body and pulled it up onto his lap. He didn't like seeing it lying there in the dirt.

She'd begun to decay, in a soft slipping fashion. The meat of her face running a little, her eyes sliding back into her sockets. She smelled high and sweet, like bacon in the sun.

Hillman wasn't sure what he was doing. A part of him wanted to rock her. A part of him wanted to tell her a fairy tale.

"Tell her a Coyote tale," Coyote said. "Women always like that."

Hillman ignored Coyote's advice.

"Hang onto her," Coyote added. "A man ought to eat what he catches."

Hillman was beat. He closed his eyes and let exhaustion club him into sleep, the dead teenage girl resting lightly on his lap. It wasn't anything sexual. He just wanted to protect her the best way he could.

As he drifted off he swore that he heard the sound of Christmas bells ringing in the wind blown branches.

#

CHAPTER 12

Awakened Into Nightmare

Hillman lay in the darkness and dreamed of himself, laying beside a campfire on a vast and windy plain.

The campfire guttered into ashes. His mouth cloyed rankly with the taste of fresh killed meat. The soft whispering flutter of seppuku moths spindled into the winking embers and hissed into final ash as their paper-thin wings hit the heat. Tiny angel moths rose up from the ashes and drifted towards the light of the hooked moon.

The little girl sat up, her face a soft vermilion veil of thin worn cotton, eyes stitched with flat black buttons.

"You don't have to do this," she said.

Hillman tried to answer, but his mouth felt as if was filled with puffballs. His words were smothered in a gargle of lint.

"Bury me here," she said. "Beside the campfire.

Anywhere that a Mi'kmaq is buried is sacred ground."

He moved his mouth open and closed but no sound escaped.

"Who are you trying to save?" she asked.

And then he leaned backwards into the arms of recollection, his thoughts winging back towards the memory of that day in the Bitter Grounds café.

He saw himself standing behind the counter, and yet somehow in front of it, as if the chrome and plexiglass surface was no more substantial than a beam of remembered sunlight.

The kid had just swung open the door, only he wasn't wearing a mask. He wore a face full of fish hooks and facial piercings, as if he'd fallen face first into a tackle shop. His hair shot up in bolts of flash-dried electricity, the color of melted crayons. He held a shotgun like a prayer stick, waving it about him and begging for money. The shotgun was chained to the kid's stomach by an iron ring that looked to be welded.

Hillman reached for his own gun, but this time there was nothing in his holster but a dead fish, limp with a glitter of metallic scales. Fish or not, he grabbed for it. There were hooks in the fish, and they latched into the meat of his hand.

The fish looked up at Hillman with bright green eyes.

The shotgun went off. Hillman felt a door open up in his belly. A beam of soft red flesh sprayed out from behind him, like wet sunlight sheening through the tunnel that had suddenly appeared in his chest.

Hillman looked down. His viscera tumbled like an unspooling coil of uncooked sausage, spilling on to the counter. For an instant in red time, Hillman stood there, trying to read the snakepit of hieroglyphics unspooling on the counter.

The viscera looked like a face with bright green

eyes. Hillman knew that it was his cancer talking, only the dream was showing him a time before he even knew about the disease. None of it made sense, but how much sense could a talking evisceration cancer-golem be expected to make?

"Listen to me Hillman," the cancer said. "I will tell you nothing but the truth. The leaves rotting into mulch know this truth. The roadkill and the carrion know this truth. We are born knowing our future."

The face of the viscera changed from a green eyed woman to an old one-eyed man. He looked a little like a worn out Gandalf, a wizened wino, with a beard of snowy white moss.

"We are born knowing we have die," the one-eyed cancer-man said. "It has always been this way. The circle of life is a big fat cancer cell. You have been born, you have to die. Life is a big bobsled ride, with one single inescapable destination. All you own is your sense of identity. Who are you, Morgan Hillman?"

There's a boy lying at his feet behind the counter. The boy wore an apron stained with ketchup. The boy reached up one pale ketchup stained hand and caught hold of Hillman's dangling viscera. He pulled himself up, one link at a time, while Hillman struggled hopelessly to free himself and push and poke the long hose of entrails back into his holed-out stomach. He stuffed and tucked in that forever of dream time, but by the time he got to the end of the entrail trail, he found that the boy's hand had somehow fused into his vulnerable flesh. Joined, melded, whole, a last link of sausage in an endless strand of gutrope.

"Who are you, Morgan Hillman?" the boy asked.

There were tears in the boy's eyes and tears on Hillman's cheek and he wondered how he could weep for someone he hardly knew. And then the boy pulled himself up and pushed his face in close against Hillman's, his breath heavy and dank and close.

By then Hillman realized he was no longer asleep, and that he was staring face to face with the big bastard.

"I know who you are," the big bastard said.

Hillman awakened into nightmare.

#

CHAPTER 13
Everybody Dies

The troll knelt there, crouched directly between Hillman and the shotgun. His false face gaped wide open, his eyes burning like a pair of blood red coals. He looked bigger than before, as if he'd gathered strength from the darkness. Maybe he had.

"Stupid," the troll growled. "Lying here in the darkness, imagining yourself safe by the fire. You have been thinking like a stone."

Hillman tried to sit up. Just that quickly, the troll was upon him, his hand about Hillman's throat. He stank like a damp basement. Mildew and mold and ancient wet granite. The boy trembled at the end of his chain like a whipped pup. Only there was something different this time. The chain looked to be imbedded into the troll's side, connected like a branch extending from the trunk of a tree.

"I came across a band of hunters once like this before," the troll said. "I caught them napping over their fire and roasted them."

"I was one of them," the hunter said, stepping out of the shadows, his musket cocked and ready to fire.

"Go ahead and shoot. Is your aim that much better, deadeye? I killed you once, and I can kill you again, right after I finish with this one."

"This time it will be different," The hunter said. "I

am in your world now, and you cannot surprise me."

The troll laughed and squeezed Hillman's neck tighter. Hillman's panic was sharp in his empty lungs, trying to breathe, trying to free himself. He was helpless.

"Do something," Lily shouted.

Hillman wondered who she was shouting at. He wished she would be quiet so that he could suffocate in peace.

The savage leaped from the shadows as quickly as a flicker of heat lightning. He drove his spear deep into the troll.

The troll turned, forcing himself up along the length of the savage's spear, stealing it with his pain and his meat, pushing himself closely enough to catch hold of the savage by both of his hawk-wired shoulders.

The savage pulled his knife and drove it in under the troll's ribs with three solid thrusts, but he might as well have struck him with a single feather for all the good it did. The troll seemed to absorb both spear and dagger, forming them into a part of himself.

Now that he had a clear aim, the hunter fired a blast at the troll. The night reeked of gunpowder and fear. As the hunter reloaded the troll pushed the savage's shoulders back and apart, tearing him wide open from stem to stern, the keel of his ribs tearing out through the darkly tanned flesh like a series of great ivory hooks.

The troll leaned over greedily, pushing his face into the cage of the savage's chest, tearing at him with his teeth. Hillman could hear the rubber texture of the savage's heart. The troll's teeth chewed into the hard heart membrane with a fat crackling sound.

Coyote leaped from the shadows atop the boy, catching the boy's throat in his jaws.

"Help, father!" the boy shouted.

The troll pulled free from the savage's chest.

What was he up to? Hillman pushed past the

distracted troll, snatching up his shotgun in midstep.

Coyote kept the boy pinned down.

The hunter raised his musket again.

"Shoot him," Coyote said. "Shoot the boy."

The troll leaped upon the hunter, yanking his musket away and smashing him to the ground with a careless heavy backhand. He turned, swinging the musket like a war club, smashing it against Coyote's skull.

Coyote fell to the ground. The boy grabbed the troll's leg.

"Shoot the boy," Coyote called out to Hillman.

The troll turned on Hillman.

One chance, Hillman thought.

"Save the boy," Lily shouted out, her voice rising above the carnage like a soft dove.

Hillman raised the shotgun, the barrel as heavy as an iron telephone pole, the triggers cutting like sharply hooked razors beneath his fingers as he squeezed, aiming for the chain.

It was a stupid play, but it was all his hands thought of in that blink of time. There was no way a shotgun had the power to shatter a chain, even that close up.

But it did.

The chain blasted apart. It was like shooting a snake. Dark fluid gouted out of it in thick spasms. The boy screamed, Lily screamed, the troll screamed. Everybody joined in on the tonsil-breaking screamathon.

Hillman lunged forward. He grabbed the boy, dragging him off of the troll. He didn't want to let go. Hillman yanked him. The troll seemed dazed, as if he'd been hit himself.

The shattered chain spurted out. Hillman grabbed it with his free hand and squeezed. It was hot and bleeding like a severed artery. The chain was alive, part of the boy. Hillman doubled it over trying to squeeze it shut like a garden hose. The boy was screaming, loud tears, like

Hillman was hurting him.

And then the troll waded in, berserk, and smashed Hillman's chest in with a single blow.

"I will gut you like a fish," the troll said.

The troll shoved his face into Hillman's opened chest.

He's going to eat my heart too, just like he ate the savage's heart, Hillman thought.

He felt all of the soft things inside his chest spill out. He tried to catch at it, like when he was shot in the coffee bar, only a thousand times worse. Everything was warm and wet and tinged with bitter sharpness.

"Hey, Red Cap!"

The troll turned, as a can of beans winged off of his forehead.

"You!" he said, staring at Lily in the girl's body. Hillman's rucksack slung over her shoulder. The molotov rested in her hands, the fuse lit and sizzling like a fat wet snake.

"Let me bake your beans for you," Lily shouted.

She threw the molotov. It shattered against the troll's face.

The troll went up like a ball of burning suet.

Hillman was mangled. Dying. This is it, he thought. I've passed over, before the cancer got me. I've finally beat the bastardly stuff. It didn't bother him. The boy would be saved. Coyote would figure out some way to fix the boy's wounds. The troll was burning. He could die, just let go, and it wouldn't hurt him one little bit. And yet he heard Big Billy Bellytumor chuckling like he hadn't had the last laugh yet.

Coyote appeared over his body, looming like the memory of a bad dream.

"Do you want to live?" Coyote asked.

Hillman didn't know what to say.

He could hear the boy screaming, loud cries:

"Daddy, daddy, daddy!"

"Yes," Hillman whispered. His voice was dry, like he hadn't had enough water. He'd lost a lot of blood.

He's not even sure he spoke the word aloud, but the coyote seemed to hear something. He bent down and pushed his muzzle against Hillman's belly. Hillman felt it hot and wet. Is that healthy, he wonders? Cold nose, healthy dog? What about coyotes?

And then the coyote began to feed.

#

CHAPTER 14
Showdown At The Bitter Grounds

Hillman fell back into a long slow red sea.

I can remember now, he thought. I can remember what happened, that night at the Bitter Grounds cafe.

It had been a slow Wednesday night. A relatively quiet time of the week.

Hillman had just come in for a cup of coffee and a slice of rhubarb pie. They bought the pie from an old Acadian woman who baked it fresh twice a week, with hydroponic rhubarb raised as a side crop in her grand daughter's marijuana greenhouse. The pie baking wasn't really a business for her, although people constantly told her that she should go professional. It was just a way for her to pass her time, which was all that Hillman was doing that night. Just killing time. He wasn't on duty. He should have been home watching the hockey game, but the players were on strike again, and to tell the truth he didn't really miss it.

Maybe that was why he'd flinched. He wasn't on duty. He didn't have his kevlar vest and his nightstick. Just an off-duty revolver tucked in a polite little holster on his belt beneath his windbreaker.

He wasn't wearing his policeman's mask.

The kid stepped in, banging the door open so that it nearly broke against the glass. He was carrying a rifle. A Lee Enfield .303. Probably something he'd stolen from his grandfather's war trophies.

Hillman recognized the rifle. His own grandfather had carried one in the war and had left it to Hillman's father who had used it as a deer rifle.

He could still hear the old man talking, his voice all wet and gravelly, like river water running over rocks, talking of the battles he'd fought and of the many times he'd gone over the top.

"Give me the money," the kid had shouted.

The clerk froze up, standing there with a hot cup of coffee in his hands, not knowing what to do.

Hillman stood there, doing his best to keep himself in between the kid and the clerk.

The bells on the door rang as the woman walked in, and all hell broke loose. The kid half turned, and Hillman went for his pistol, and the kid turned back and fired a shot off, catching Hillman in the meat of his shoulder. His own shot went astray from the bullet's impact, and it caught the woman straight through her eye.

Only it happened fast. Hillman squeezed the trigger, and the boy's rifle barked, and Hillman's arm burned, and the woman winked at him. She turned from the impact of the shot, stumbled towards Hillman, dead already, but legs working like forgotten clockwork engines winding down.

She fell against the boy as he ran for the door.

The boy ran from the cafe, dropping his rifle. A squad car caught him two blocks away, still running, covered in the dead woman's blood.

When they found Hillman he was praying over the coffee counter, over the body of the dead clerk who'd caught what was left of the heavy rifle bullet after it tore through Hillman.

He turned and looked at the two policemen standing in the doorway. He stood there, smiling with a coffee mug in one hand and a pot in the other, pouring without looking.

"How may I help you?" he'd asked. "How may I help you?"

The coffee spilled over the lip of the mug and onto the counter and down.

"How may I help you?"

#

CHAPTER 15
We Can Rebuild You

Evisceration is an amazing sensation. Feeling your guts slipping away, like a loose chain unspooling.

It's funny. You'd think he'd be scared. Isn't that what's supposed to happen when you lose your guts? You get scared?

You run away?

He felt the coyote's teeth, neat and sharp, working into his cancer, chewing each bit of Hillman's disease. A part of him wanted to ask about the coyote's dental plan. How often he'd been to the dentist in the last three years? Had he had all his shots?

Hillman giggled. The sound terrified him, a high pitched wet giggle, so much like the coyote.

"I lost my coat once," Coyote said. "Did I tell you that? Sure, I remember. You look worse than I did, though."

"Thanks."

"I remember this time I was watching the alder leaves fall in the autumn. They looked so pretty dancing down with the wind. I figured that if I could fall like that, all soft and pretty, I could catch me a whole lot of women. So I asked them leaves how it was done and they told me it was easy. All I had to do was to climb up in a tree as high as I could get, and then just fall. So I tried that, climbed up high into the alder tree and until the branches were bending like grass beneath my feet and then I launched myself off. It wasn't pretty when I fell. Pieces of me, all mud-pied over the ground. I picked myself up and kept walking, kept travelling."

Hillman watched. He wondered if the coyote should be talking with his mouth so full of Hillman's insides. Wasn't it bad manners, to talk with a full mouth while cannibalizing the dead?

"I never did learn how to fall like that."

Could it even be considered cannibalism? Coyote was a coyote, and Hillman was a corpse. It was kind of a natural development when you thought about it that way.

"I remember another time, I'd climbed up to the moon on a spider's web. Did it with my eyes closed, not looking down. Come to getting back down I wasn't so certain. So I asked the spider and he said I just needed to step on down, to keep my eyes tight closed, and not think about the ground until I reached it."

"Do you do everything you're ever told?" Hillman gritted.

"Not usually, but I did that time," Coyote answered. "Let me tell you the moon is a lot higher up than an alder. I hit the ground hard, and died for a while. The beetles crawled up and the ants crawled out, and they ate my meat and my fur blew away with the wind. Later on a squirrel come up and jammed a bright green pebble where my eye used to be. Then a blue jay popped a little acorn in where the other eye used to be. Right then I could see where I was going, and once that had happened I sort of pulled myself together, kept walking, kept travelling."

"Death's just no place to stop for too long. There's no goodbye that lasts forever. Your heart is a drum that don't know how to stop beating. All you can do is to keep on walking, keep on travelling."

The coyote kept working on Hillman's disease, mealing it down into a thick clottish puree, grinding it, straining it, each tooth working like a mouthful of mortars and pestles. Not swallowing, just holding it in his mouth. Letting it simmer. Percolate.

What's cooking, Hillman thought, barely clenching his teeth against another giggle. What's cooking?

"You ran. You got shot, and then you ran, hiding behind the mask of a coffee server. You didn't fool anybody but yourself. They knew who you were, they could read your identification. You ran and you hid. There's no shame in that. Everybody runs sometimes, it's why *Kji-kinap* gave us legs. But after you've run you've got to come back. You've got to let it out and come back."

And then with great deliberation and delicacy the coyote sicked up the entire mess over Hillman's wounds, being careful to cover every inch of Hillman's body.

Oh that's just nasty, Hillman thought.

The coyote began licking him. It should have tickled. It should have disgusted.

Does this mean we're going steady, Hillman wondered? In his brain he kept seeing a vision of Lucy being licked by Snoopy. Eeew, dog germs. Get some antiseptic. Get some iodine.

He felt the coyote's tongue, moving and prodding him.

He felt the regurgitated cancer, cloying and congealing and absorbing him, forming a kind of organic armor.

"Get up," Coyote said. "You have remembered all that you need to know. You are a warrior and you are ready to do battle."

At the last of it Coyote reached down with something shiny in his mouth, like a star, like a hook, and placed it in Hillman's brand new armor.

It hung there, stuck fast.

A policeman's badge.

#

CHAPTER 16
How Many Times Can You Kill A God?

The troll stumbled against a cedar tree, then leaned on it as the world dizzied past.

She'd surprised him.

He felt the anger boiling over. He let it take him and uprooted the cedar tree from the dry autumn soil.

Where had she come from?

No longer supported by the tree, he stumbled forward until he caught at another tree. A birch, tall and strong, but not strong enough. He pushed it over with a single shove, then leaned and panted in unexpected exhaustion.

What was he doing? Would it help at all to level the forest? He needed to calm down. He was just so angry. She'd hurt him with that fire bottle, but that wasn't what he was really angry about.

He was angry over her. Hurting him again, in front of that coyote. That hurt far worse than any mere burn.

She'd hurt him once before with that damned coyote. He'd worn another face then, but the troll recognized him just the same. He recognized the stink. He'd smelled it on her, after she'd been with him. That mangy bastard, having her, tainting her with his seed and his scent.

"Damn!"

He wheeled about and clotheslined a small spruce, end over ending it into a thatch of scruffy alders. Momentum carried him into the dirt. He lay there on his hands and knees, bowed and broken, his lungs heaving like billowing sails.

Everything slipped slowly away.

He was dying. The boy would die with him. He thought he'd been safe, putting his heart in the boy's chest and then linking them with a soul chain, but the little man's gun had ruined everything. How could he have known to shoot the chain?

That damned coyote. Loki or whatever he called himself these days. He must have whispered the troll's secret to the man, the same way he'd whispered it to old one-eye, after worming it out of the woman with his damnably persuasive tongue and penis.

Damn it! He'd cared for her. How could she be so ungrateful?

He dug his hands deep into the dead needled mulch, working his thick fingers until he touched something cold and familiar.

Stone. Not the north stone, not the snake stone, but stone nonetheless. He leeched its cold stone strength into himself, drawing at the eternal memory of the rock.

Yes. That was better.

He felt his vigor return.

He would fight on. The man was dead. He'd tasted his heart's blood. All that stood between him and his heart was the coyote and the woman.

He would finish them both. First the coyote, pulling his legs and tail and snout from their sockets. Then the woman. Let her try and hide in that little girl's body. He would pull her out and kill her, again and again. You could kill a spirit many times, before making it permanent.

He wondered how many times he could kill a god.

Even a dirty insignificant dog god like Coyote.

It would be his pleasure and privilege to find out, again and again and again, for as long as it took.

He drew further on the strength of the rock, growing stronger and angrier with every foul breath he took.

#

CHAPTER 17
Metaphysics For Dummies

Hillman lay there in his living cancer armor, feeling stronger by the minute. Lily and the boy busied themselves by the fire. Coyote knelt over him.

"You saved me," Hillman said, touching the black chitinous armour, feeling it warm and sticky beneath his fingertips. "You really are a god."

Coyote laughed. "That's what I've been telling you, isn't it?"

"But you saved me. Brought me back from the dead. You are god."

Coyote shook his head ruefully.

"Not god. Not *the* god. *A* god, that's what I am. And I didn't bring you back from the dead. I just caught you before you fell in too far."

"I don't understand," Hillman said. "Isn't it the same?"

"*He's* the one that's into bringing dead back into life. He's your original recycler with Lazarus and all of that shit. I'm not into any of that. Dead is dead. I make the trip any chance I get, because it's a hell of a ride, but I'll be damned if I'm bringing anyone back with me."

Coyote sneezed.

"See," he went on. "I'm allergic to the idea. Zombies scare the poop out of me."

Hillman couldn't resist asking, "So, do you know him?"

"Who?"

"*Him.*" Hillman said, pointing solemnly upwards. It was hard to point with fingers that felt like mutant cucumbers. "God."

"Name dropper. Sure I know Him. He makes a hell of a martini," Coyote said, still examining the flea. "I just don't like to talk that much about him since he retired."

"Retired?"

"Sure. You don't believe all of that guff about him dying, do you?"

Hillman shrugged, which was even harder than pointing.

"So where'd he go?" he asked. "Tahiti? Florida? Mars?"

"New Mexico. I don't think he ever learned to like the water. He drives around the desert in an all-terrain Winnebago, big as Utah. No cares, no commitments, just the view of the windscreen and whatever else he chooses to see. It's good to be the King."

"You're kidding me. A Winnebago?"

"Yup. Big as Utah. Can you imagine all of the fossil juice a rig like that must guzzle? Talk about your global warming. I told him to keep the Harley, but do you think He'd listen to me? Too many bugs in his teeth, says He. Ha! Protein, says I."

He popped the flea into his mouth, closing his teeth with an exaggerated bear trap snap.

Hillman was confused.

"I thought you said that you and the great spirit built the world."

"Built *a* world. Note the indefinite article. There are more worlds than this one, white man. More gods, too. My father's mansion has many rooms. Listen up, this here's a crash course in metaphysics. Everything happens together, just like lanes in a mega-cosmic-multi-reality freeway, you just shift one lane over and you've shifted into another realm of existence. That's called possibility, learn to embrace it."

Hillman didn't understand. "So if there's more than one god, why doesn't one of them do something about this troll? Isn't he evil enough for them?"

Coyote laughed, nearly spitting out the flea. "That'd be too much like trying to cure you of your own shadow."

"I don't get it."

"Listen. Existence is a giant crystal, cut into nine billion facets. God stares into the heart of existence and his reflection is broken into nine billion reflections. I'm one of them, you're another, and so is the troll."

He closed one eye, and stared at Hillman with the other.

"So when do we hunt him down?" Hillman asked.

"What do you mean *we*, white man?"

#

CHAPTER 18
Pissed Off and Pissed On

Coyote kept on staring, refusing to say a word.

"I've picked up his trail," said the hunter, stepping out of the darkness. "Glad to see you're still alive."

Hillman looked down at his armadillo hide of raw cancer.

"I'm not sure if you could call this alive, but I'm damn well still kicking. What about you? I thought you were dead, for sure."

The hunter skinned back his lips in a grin. "It's hard to kill a dead man."

Hillman gestured over to the remains of the savage.

"He doesn't seem to be moving."

"I said it was hard," the hunter answered. "Not impossible."

"The troll ate his heart," Coyote added.

"Well listen to that, he can speak," Hillman said.

Coyote ignored his sarcasm. "The heart holds all of a man's fire and spirit. Kill it and the body dies. He would have eaten both of your hearts, if the girl hadn't thrown that firebomb."

Lily stepped forward from tending the fire. She held the boy close. "The girl didn't help," she said. "The woman did. The woman saved your damned asses."

Coyote rolled his eyes.

"So are we ready?" the hunter said. "Do we hunt him?"

"He doesn't want to go," Hillman said, pointing at Coyote.

Everyone looked expectantly at Coyote.

"We don't need to hunt the troll," Coyote explained. "We've got what we need right here."

"What's that?" Hillman asked.

"The boy. He's carrying the troll's heart. That's why your gunshots didn't hurt him. Kill the boy, and this all will be over."

Lily stepped in front of the boy.

"You can't kill him," she said.

"He's dying all ready. Just look at him."

It was true. The boy's face was pale, his breathing labored. If the dead *had* learned to walk, they would look a lot like him.

"We've got no choice," Coyote went on, appealing to the hunter.

The hunter stepped beside Lily.

"Hey wait a minute," Coyote protested. "You're with me."

"I'm with her," Hunter said. "You stand alone."

Hillman watched this play out. He thought of the lovemaking the night before. He looked at Lily. Had she planned this?

Hillman raised his shotgun, and pointed it at Coyote. It was hard, getting his fingers in around the trigger, but he managed it all the same.

"You're supposed to be some kind of god, aren't you? Aren't gods supposed to protect their people?"

Coyote snorted. "That's not me. That's some other god. I'm Coyote, the trickster. Coyote the thief. Steal your woman, your purse, your very skin off of your back, that's me. Coyote."

"Trust you to be untrustworthy, is that what you're telling me?"

"At least I know what I am," Coyote said.

"I remember a lot about what I am. This skin gave that back to me," Hillman said, tapping his badge. "Protect and serve, I remember that much."

Coyote had enough.

"Last chance. Are you going to shoot him?"

The hunter raised his musket.

Hillman moved to protect the boy, just in case. He didn't think the musket blast could penetrate his cancerous hide.

Only the hunter wasn't pointing his musket at the boy. He was pointing it at Coyote.

"I think he's right," the hunter said. "I don't think we need to kill the boy. I don't *want* to kill a boy."

"Damn," Coyote swore. "Just when I was beginning to like you."

He inhaled, puffing up his cheeks like he was trying to dry swallow a pair of bowling balls. Then he blew out at the hunter. The hunter dissipated like a cloud of dark smoke before a heavy wind.

"Like that trick?" Coyote asked Hillman. "I learned it from a wolf."

Hillman swallowed hard. He was standing up to a god who could probably huff and puff up a hurricane.

To hell with that. He'd stood up to cancer, he could stand up to this.

"You were going to kill yourself last time I checked," said Coyote.

"This seems as good a way to die as any."

Lily picked up a fallen branch, hefting it like a war club, and stood next to Hillman.

"Watch the boy," Hillman warned.

"Watch yourself," she said right back.

Hillman smiled. Then he turned back to Coyote, and took a step forward.

"You have the right to remain silent," Hillman said.

Coyote laughed silently.

Hillman put his shotgun up to his shoulder.

"Anything you say can and will be used against you."

Coyote threw back his head and laughed louder. With each laugh he grew a little larger.

"You have the right to speak to an attorney and to have an attorney present during questioning, if you so desire. If you cannot afford an attorney, one will be provided for you."

Coyote kept laughing and growing.

Hillman pumped a shell into the shotgun. "Do you understand each and every one of these rights as I've presented them to you?"

Coyote swelled up all at once to the size of a mutant sabretooth, opening his jaws and roaring loud enough to give a lion an earache. Hillman jammed the shotgun into Coyote's open throat.

"Why don't we see if you can gargle buckshot?"

Coyote clamped his teeth down hard around the barrel and yanked the gun out of Hillman's grasp. He leaped up like an excited six hundred pound puppy and knocked Hillman down to the dirt.

This is it, Hillman thought. I finally get to die, right when I've decided I don't really want to.

Lily smashed her branch over Coyote's skull, but he ignored her effort. He pushed his snout down close enough for Hillman to taste Coyote snot.

"Piss on you," Coyote said.

And then he turned around and did just that. Cocked his leg and pissed on Hillman's cancer-coated chest.

Hillman was surprised at how ordinary the coyote's piss was. He'd expected it to be something magical, like radioactive lemonade lava, but it was just simple urine.

And it stank.

He lay there in the dirt, pissed on and pissed off.

"Fuck you, tar baby," Coyote said.

And then he turned and walked out of the camp.

#

CHAPTER 19
Hunting For Trouble, And Finding It

He was on his own. No hunter, no Coyote, just the dead woman following behind.

Wasn't this just how he'd started out? He'd come full circle. Life turns this way, every time. Just when you think you've got past something, there it was just a little further up the road. The world kept on turning and no matter where you started out from and where you were bound for, sooner or later you came around full circle.

Only this time they had a boy to think about. Lily had tied a rag about the chain, and some of her herbs. She wasn't sure if it would work for long. Hillman didn't know either. All he knew was it was time to hunt.

He spotted a footprint about as deep and wide as a

shoebox. Here a shattered pine tree and there a broken boulder. The troll wasn't exactly making it hard for him. Hell, he probably wanted to be found. Just letting the chase go on for the hell of it.

Bastard.

Still, it wasn't easy. Police academy hadn't trained him much in the ways of woodland tracking. He tried to remember everything he'd learned in Boy Scouts. He tried to tap into his racial memories, but the only race memory he could unearth was a flash snapshot of himself finishing dead last at a grade school track and field meet.

He hadn't really learned to run until later in his life when he'd served in the reserves. He'd hated the needless discipline, so he'd joined the police academy. There was just as much discipline, but catching criminals seemed to make more sense to him.

He'd served fifteen years as a police officer. Then came the showdown at the Bitter Grind. They'd walked him out of there and into the psych ward. It had taken him two years before they believed he'd come out of it.

And then the cancer, and then this.

He looked back at the dead woman and the boy. The boy was sniffling, like he'd caught a cold.

"So where do you fit in all of this?" Hillman asked.

"Behind you," Lily said. "Always behind you."

It sounded sweet when she said it, but Hillman knew better.

"Bullshit," Hillman swore, pushing past another fallen tree. "The troll knows you. The coyote knows you. All I ever did was shoot you, by accident. Where the hell do you fit in?"

She was quiet for a few minutes. Hillman let her stew as they walked. The forest seemed to hang and listen. This far into the woods it could have been anywhere, at any time. Modern technology disappeared this far back in the woods. Calculators turned into pinecones, color televisions faded into sunsets, and cars took root.

"Okay," she said.

Hillman kept walking, tracking and listening.

"I was in love with Coyote and married to the troll."

That brought him to a halt.

"Come again?"

"It happened a long time ago, long before the Christ child was even in fashion. I was the troll's bride. He'd stolen me as a child from my parents' home, raised me, and then one day made me his bride."

Hillman clenched his fists. "That son of a bitch."

Lily shrugged. "I don't know if it was that simple. I believe he had feelings for me. I did for him. He'd raised me and protected me. I knew more about him than I'd known about my parents."

"You sound like you had feelings for him."

She shrugged. "Sometimes we choose our gods, and sometimes they choose us." She nodded at the boy. "Same as him. That troll has been his whole world. Now you've come between them."

"I rescued him."

Lily shook her head. "Sometimes it just isn't that easy."

"You came between us too," the boy said, staring at Lily. "That's why I freed you. So he wouldn't love you. So he'd love me."

"He's talking to the girl," Lily said. "Not me. Just the body I'm wearing."

Hillman wondered about the truth of that, but he couldn't tell for sure. He nodded, turned, and kept walking. They were closer now, he could feel it. They'd been tracking for hours, yet Hillman knew it wouldn't be much longer.

"So where did Coyote come in?" he asked.

She smiled, almost wistfully.

"He was called Loki, back then. He never really was

bad, at first. Just another thread in Odin's web, that old one-eyed bastard."

A crow burst from the shadows with a gunshot flapping of its wings. He rose to the trees and sat up there watching them.

"The kingpin, eh?"

"That's one way of putting it. Odin wanted the troll out of the picture, because he was afraid that he'd pose too much of a threat in the coming battle between Asgard and the evil ones. So he sent Loki in to find his weakness. And Loki found me."

"So he seduced you."

Lily looked embarrassed. "He could talk," she said. "A silver tongue. I'm afraid I listened too well."

"Well he's gone now. It's just us against the troll."

They stepped from the trees, and there they were. The ruins of the campfire. The remains of savage, his ribs now grown and twisted into wooden roots and shadows, not a sign that there'd once been a body there.

And there, standing by the campfire, was the troll.

They'd come full circle.

The troll came running at them.

Hillman raised the shotgun.

#

CHAPTER 20

Tar Baby Death Throes

Pump, squeeze, pump, squeeze.

Hillman emptied the shotgun in a pointless ejaculation of lead and gunpowder. It didn't seem to do much against the troll's hardened hide, but it still felt good, the pumping and booming and the recoil kicking with apparent purpose beneath his arm.

As the troll got closer Hillman swung the shotgun like a long club, hard against the troll's neck. It bent and curved. Hillman thought it looked prettier than it had. More natural, like a wave or a branch.

The troll tore into Hillman, swinging a haymaker right that impacted against Hillman's ribs. The bastard hit him so hard that Hillman worried they'd spring loose. They'd just been grown back, and he wasn't that confident in the cancer crazy-glue the coyote had used on him. The cancer armor made him tougher now, maybe even invulnerable, but he felt the blow all the same.

The boy pulled free of Lily's grasp and ran at the troll. Lily ran after him.

Using his cancer-armor strength, Hillman snapped a branch the thickness of a man's leg from the crotch of a nearby poplar. He smashed the wood against the side of the troll's skull. The branch shattered ineffectually into a flurry of toothpicks. Hillman might as well be taking on a full-grown Sherman tank with a handful of limp pasta.

Lily grabbed the boy again, holding him harder.

The troll hammered another blow into Hillman's gut. Hillman felt that too. The bastard was getting through. His technique sucked, but he was stronger than god.

"Daddy!" the boy hollered, struggling to try and free himself from Lily's grasp.

"Give me the boy," the troll snarled.

"Fuck you," Hillman swore, landing a heavy left into the troll's rock-hard belly. He followed through nicely; he probably looked as pretty as hell, but he couldn't touch the big fucker.

The troll swung back at him with a high hard overhand that slammed against Hillman's chest, directly on the spot where Coyote had pissed. Hillman felt the cancer hide giving way beneath the troll's assault, like a sticky kind of tar, sucking the troll's iron hard fist into itself.

"Now I've got you," Hillman said with a nasty laugh.

The troll moved deeper into Hillman's chest, stepping into his swing, forcing his arm through the cancer-armor. This was a big mistake. Hillman wasn't trapping the troll. Hillman had trapped himself around the troll's grip. He was as much a prisoner as the big bastard was.

"I can feel you, inside you, feel your insides turning into glue," the troll said. "I can feel your heart."

Hillman willed his heart to squeeze the troll's hand and hold it fast, like a milk bottle monkey trap.

The troll swung another blow with his other arm. Hard and deep.

Both of his hands were sunk deep into Hillman's chest.

He was stuck fast.

"Take the boy!" Hillman shouted.

"He's mine," the troll said.

"Not now," Hillman said. "I can hold you like this for a long time. Maybe forever. How long until you starve to death? How long until you rot?"

"You don't know what you're doing," the troll growled.

"I wonder," Hillman said, pushing himself forward, trying to draw the troll deeper into himself. "I wonder if I can't suck you right up inside me like the world's ugliest strand of spaghetti?"

The troll opened his mouth wider, pushing his face teeth-first out of his skin mask.

"Maybe I can swallow you whole."

Hillman gritted his teeth and pushed closer, trying to limbo dance himself away from the troll's teeth while drawing the troll's body closer in.

"Suck, swallow, what's the difference? We're all going to have a damn good time."

The boy screamed. Lily was holding him with all of her spirit might. The troll's teeth were getting closer. They would soon be close enough to rip Hillman's face off, and Hillman had arrived at the point of view where he just didn't give a good god damn.

And just at that moment, a voice from the wild clear blue howled out, "Tar baby sit, and don't say 'nuthin!"

#

CHAPTER 21

Always Pack Your Sunscreen

Hillman looked up and saw Coyote, grown impossibly large, swooping down with the sun in his mouth, looking a lot like the world's largest and ugliest Labrador retriever.

"Thought you were safe, didn't you? Hiding under that big red cap, in that big shady truck in the dark old woods," Coyote called out around the mouthful of sun.

Troll looked wildly around, searching for a chance at escape. His hat fell to the ground behind him.

"Hold him still, white man. I think he finally sees the light."

It was an impossible sight. The sun drawing closer, like a great yellow ball, like something a five year old might have colored and a moonstruck graphic artist might have animated. A story, in the mouth of a storyteller, Coyote had sung down the sun.

He flew closer. Hillman felt the cancerous tar on his body bubbling and melting. Was he going to evaporate, burn up, or just fade away? He couldn't be certain, but he knew one thing. That damned troll liked it a whole lot less than he did.

The troll looked up into Hillman's eyes. For just an instant he was no longer a monster. He was just a frightened dark reflection.

Like a shadow.

And then he was gone. Burned up, melted, or vanished.

Just gone.

The boy pulled free of Lily, and grabbed the troll's fallen red hat.

Coyote crashed to the ground, letting the sun fly free. It lofted upwards like a released yellow birthday balloon. Up, up and then gone.

Burned up, melted or vanished.

Coyote lay there in the dirt.

Hillman crawled over to him.

Coyote looked like ten hells. His legs were snapped like kindling, his skin dry and desiccated. There were burns about his mouth, like fat black greasy worms crawling about through the skin down into the rotted gums.

And he was laughing.

"Are you dead?" Hillman asked.

"Dead? Ha! I am Coyote. I am the rag and the thorn and the bone. I am the scar and the saguaro and the lightning-struck pine. I am the rock and I am the wind, I have died and been reborn, I have felt the eagle tearing at my liver, and I keep on walking, keep on wandering."

He chuckled softly, a saw rasping over sun-dried wood.

"And I never did learn how to fall."

And then the Coyote was gone.

The boy plunked the troll's red hunting cap down about his ears. It covered his face like a red plaid mask.

#

CHAPTER 22
We'll Burn That Bridge When We Get There

It was very hot that October and the scientists blamed it on global warming, and the activists blamed it on the politicians, and the politicians said that there was nothing that a little tax raise wouldn't cure.

The sun seemed bigger and brighter that year, and if you looked closely you could still see a few ragged tooth marks that Coyote had left behind.

And everyone dreamed of the cool night moon.

The wind had a soft haunting howl, the dirt stank of dung, and the color of the leaves were running dark dirty red, like coyote blood.

The boy led Hillman and Lily to the troll's cabin. It was hard to find, hiding inside of a large granite rock.

Hillman stayed out of sight. His cancer didn't seem to bother him, now that he was wearing it on the outside. He didn't hunt or fish, although he had both gun and fishing gear. He lived off of tinned beans and spaghetti that he liberated from an overturned tractor trailer. Sometimes he mixed them both together in the same fry pan. They tasted that good that way.

He and Lily and the boy took long walks in the darkness. The few times they were spotted, produced an interesting variation upon the standard Bigfoot anecdote. Tales of a Maritime Bigfoot who was into white slavery found their way into a few seedy tabloids, and then promptly vanished.

And then one night as Hillman, the boy and Lily walked through the remains of the final battlefield, they saw something very strange. A great bridge, like a long dark rainbow, arcing over the hillside, originating from the place where Coyote died.

"It's the bridge," the boy said. "That's what the troll guarded. Odin kept him there, with the promise that one day he might let the troll across."

"What do you think?" Hillman asked Lily.

"I think that wherever a Mi'kmaq is buried, is sacred ground."

Hillman wasn't certain if she was talking about Coyote, or the hunter.

"Do you think we should cross it?" he asked.

"Why not?" Lily said. "I've never been to Valhalla before."

The boy nodded eagerly, grinning from beneath his troll-father's red cap.

Feeling a little like there ought to be a scarecrow and a tin woodsman in their midst, Hillman stepped onto the bridge. Lily walked beside him.

He looked back.

The boy was standing at the foot of the bridge, leaning into thin air, like a mime in a high breeze.

"Come on, slowpoke," Hillman called.

It was no good. The boy couldn't move. Hillman clambered back down. Caught hold of him, but it was a futile as trying to drag the Statue of Liberty with a key chain. The boy couldn't budge.

"I can't go," the boy said. "Someone has to stay and watch the bridge."

Hillman looked down at the boy, then back at Lily. She didn't say a word, but he could hear her talking as clearly as a bell.

He picked the hat up off the boy and plunked it down over his head.

"Go on," he said to the boy.

The boy stood there staring up at him.

"Go on," Hillman repeated. "Don't make me ask twice."

The boy headed up the bridge, the remnants of the

soul chain dragging like a soft metal tail. Lily waved goodbye sadly.

"Save the boy," Hillman whispered.

And then they were gone.

He straightened the red hat upon his head. It seemed a good fit.

He looked up, watching for the morning sun, feeling the cancer in his hide slowly stiffening to stone.

#

Epilogue
A Highway Never Really Ends

Further down south, alongside of a New Mexican highway, a lone mangy coyote limped down the road.

He had to be the world's ugliest coyote, with bits of fur charred black, and scars running up and down his mangy hide. He was grinning through teeth that had been broken, and his lips were seared the color of dying poppies.

A Winnebago, as large as Utah, rolled by sounding a fat klaxon horn.

The coyote stood up on its hind legs and hooked a hopeful thumb into the wind.

The driver, a large fat man in a Hawaiian shirt that looked to be made out of patches of stratosphere and mingled aurora borealis, blew a long and admirable raspberry from between his fat puckered lips.

The Coyote extended a single finger skyward.

HAMMURABI ROAD

"Trains ain't all that trained,
no matter how hard you lay your tracks."
(old railroad saying)

All roads lead to roam.
Steve Vernon

1

The moon was a stone's throw away from the Jack Pine Stretch and the lights of the town were nothing but a distant memory and the three of us were bunched together in the front seat of the pickup on account of the back seat being crammed full of Tyree. He was kicking up some, trying to shuck himself out of the duct tape, snare wire and rope we'd tangled him up in, but other than that he wasn't making much of a sound. The gag helped some and fear of retribution did the rest.

"Moose are the worst," I said.

"Worse than cows?" Donny asked.

The thing about Donny was he didn't always care about hearing the answer. To him talking was a little like table tennis. The object of the game was to snap that ball right back at the other guy just as fast and as hard as you can. Donny had an incurable habit of asking questions because it pretty well guaranteed an answer. Words just felt good coming out of his mouth, I guess. I didn't mind. Donny looked up to me and made no secret about it. I did my best to live up to his respect. Bert and Ernie couldn't have done it any better.

"Worse than bears," I said. "Usually a moose will just bounce, but man alive when they get their hooves tangled up in the tracks the engine will drag them a mile before letting go. You've got to hose their carcasses out of the locomotive's wheel trucks. I'm telling you that nothing stinks like dead moose. Not even Irvin."

Donny liked that. He grinned me that Donny smile of his. Half cocked to one side, all bright and innocent. Looking at that Donny smile I knew that nothing could ever change between us. Donny and I were arguing about what kind of track-kill stank the worst after it had been pile-driver-pureed by a half a mile of freight train. It happened more often than you might think.

"You're sure about that, are you?" Donny asked.

"Sure as shooting," I replied.

"Shooting isn't sure," Donny pointed out. "Sometimes people miss."

Donny had a point in his own weird kind of way. That was Donny's magic. He wasn't slow or retarded or whatever you want to call it. He just had a different way of looking at things, was all.

"You know what I mean Donny."

"I know what you figure you mean, but you're only guessing. There's three sides to every story," Donny said. "Yours, mine and the truth."

I smiled and nodded, preferring not to argue, but I did know what I was talking about. In my twenty years of railroading I'd shovelled and swept and hosed more track-kill from off of the CNR rails than the rest of this pickup truck combined, including Tyree. There was something magnetic in those rails that called for the kill more surely than the north wind calls the wandering wild goose home.

"Do you think there are any bears out here?" Donny asked nervously.

Donny gets antsy when you mention bears, even the Winnie the Pooh stuffed kind. He's got what you might call a history with bears.

"All of the bears will be down to the town dump by now, feeding off of the weekend leavings," I said. "And here we are out here, missing the show."

It was as true as train tracks. The bears hang around down at the old town dump and waited all week for the garbage trucks to roll in with something good to eat. It was easy pickings, sure, but I think it was also just something for them to do. Just the same way we'd go up there to the dump on the weekends and watch the bears picking through the garbage. Sometimes life was just a way of making the time go past.

Donny had his own way of passing the time. He used to go down to the dump with a pellet rifle when he was a kid and even older, taking pot-shots at the bears. He liked to plink those bears with his bee-bee's, figuring they were so damn big they couldn't even feel it. Except one day one of them bears took it into its shaggy mind to prove Donny wrong. I never saw a grown man climb a tree so fast. Too bad the bear could climb too. If I hadn't pulled the pickup truck under the tree while Donny jumped for it the story might have ended up with what was left of Donny coming out of the bear's asshole in slow dark chunks. Ever since then Donny just didn't care much for bears.

I guess I could understand that, just fine.

"Dead skunk smells worse than bear." Donny looked nervously out the window, as if he expected Smokey the Bear to come running up from out of the darkness to break the window glass with a well-swung shovel. "Way worse. Don't you think so, Irvin?"

"Shut up and let me drive," Irvin said, speed-jittering his Players filterless from one corner of his mouth to the other and back in an irritating kind of fuck-you-and-the-caboose-you-rode-in-on way. Irvin was like that. Dead focussed on the task at hand. He didn't care for distractions of any sort, which was understandable given that we were driving down a dirt trail in the dark of a moonless night with our headlights turned off. That Irvin had good eyes, I guess. He leaned right over the steering wheel, his face practically jammed up against the windshield glass, just staring into the darkness and driving at it straight on.

"What the hell are you steering by?" I asked. "You sure as shit can't see a thing."

"I can see the starlight glinting off of the rail tracks," Irvin said. "That's all of the compass I'll ever need."

I looked hard. It was true. You could see the rails

glinting in the darkness. I guess the trail was always there if you looked hard enough for something to follow. Maybe that's what the railroad tracks were for. To let us know where we were going and where we had been.

"I still think a cow is worse," Donny said. "When their guts blow up and all of that fart gas honks out. I seen two cows get it once, up around west of Wawa. They were humping on the track and I guess they didn't hear the train coming. They got creamed while they were creaming. Pretty damn funny, I think."

"Wouldn't that have been a bull and a cow?" I asked. "If they were doing what I think they were doing?"

"I don't know," Donny said with a shrug. "Maybe they were lesbian cows."

I nodded. It almost made sense if you didn't stop too long to think about it. Most things did.

"Scratch a cow, find a lesbian," Irvin observed. "Pretty girls put it out the best."

Irvin was always the deep thinker of our bunch.

The three of us had been together since we were kids. Irvin had six years on us, but he'd flunked grade twelve twice before his old man got him hooked up on the section gang. Irvin learned a whole lot more from diesel and steel than he ever learned in school. He followed the rails and he never looked back.

"Man, there's nothing worse than cow farts," Donny said. "They stink like rotten grass gas."

"Rotten ass grass gas," I suggested, stringing one more box car onto his line.

"Rotten ass grass gas, passing fast," Donny elaborated, with a silly little giggle. Then we both started to laugh. It wasn't that funny, but the giggling and the gag-cracking helped keep our minds off of what we were getting set to do.

"I'm trying to drive here," Irvin announced, in a louder than usual voice. "Do you fellows mind holding it down, or am I going to have duct tape the two of you shut up as well?"

We both shut up. Not that we usually listened all that hard to what Irvin had to say, but we both knew what he was thinking about. It had been our buddies who had died in that Hammer Abbey Hotel fire, and we had plenty to beef about with Tyree for setting the blaze, but it had been Irvin's big brother Gilbert who died there as well. Blood counted more than anybody's buddy in any book you cared to name, and some that had no name at all.

There wasn't proof that Tyree did it, but the whole town knew it as a fact. Tyree had been royally pissed at the hotel ever since they threw him out for scratching up the snooker table the time he used a leaf rake for a pool cue. So I guess everybody just plain figured that Tyree had set the fire, and that was all the judge and jury we needed in these here parts.

The real truth was that most folks just didn't care for Tyree's family. You see, Tyree came from Norman Township, where the roads were all dirt and you got your water from an iron pump. That wasn't all that bad in itself. Indeed, the fact was that nearly half of the local crew came from Norman township, but Tyree's family came from the side of Norman that folks on the other side of Norman loved to talk about the most, the wrong side of the wrong side of the tracks, so when somebody dumped a couple of quarts of gasoline in the backroom of the Hammer Abbey Railroad Hotel and threw in a lit book of matches after it, Tyree was the first usual suspect to be considered.

Now the Hammer Abbey wasn't that much as hotels went. The rooms were small and you could smell what your neighbour ate for his supper at 3am in the morning when the night farts kicked in, but it was where the traveling men would hang their hats. The rooms were cheap and fairly clean and it was ice cube handy to the bootlegger's shack. So when it went up in blazes folks around here decided that they'd miss it.

Still, there wasn't all that much in the way of material evidence so the courts and the cops didn't do much about it. The police just shrugged and Pontius Pilated their donut-stained hands into the air. Life moved on and the sun kept going up and down and the trains kept rolling.

So it was up to us.

We drove on in silence for a minute or two. That was about as long of a silence as Donny could hold on to.

"Cow farts are bad," Donny allowed. "A piggery smells worse, though. You ever drive past one?"

"There's a pig farm out by Coniston," I said. "You can smell the damn thing for miles."

"Ain't that funny?" Donny said. "Pig shit smells so bad but bacon smells so good. How's that work, you figure?"

"It's the smoke that does it," I allowed. "They smoke and salt the pork. That smoke drives all of the pig shit out of meat, I reckon."

"I wish to hell somebody would smoke and salt you, Hanny," Irvin growled. "Maybe that'd do something about all of the shit you're so full of."

That was my name, Hanny. It was short for Hanlan, my grandpa's name. My folks gave the name to me back when I was born and unable to protect myself from such abuses, figuring I could hold onto it after grandpa finally died. That's how it worked in our family. Names were handed down like old clothes in a kind of living memorial. Just as soon as somebody grew out of one name somebody else got to wear it.

I figured on saving my money and buying myself a brand new name someday. I had in mind something snazzy, like Trick Magnet H. Flash, but first I figured I'd better learn how to rap. I figured that if I could just change my name it might just change my entire life outlook. I might grow a longer dick, and go up a whole tax bracket, and maybe even bag me a cheerleader or two.

"I smoked Labrador tea once," Donny said. "It didn't do a thing for me. I never tried smoking bacon before."

"You're not supposed to smoke Labrador tea," I said. "You drink it. It's good for farts – not that you need any help in that department. Your back door works just fine and dandy."

It was true. Given enough hard boiled eggs and home brewed beer Donny could single-handedly lay down a counter-barrage on any Saturday bean supper you cared to name. It was kind of his calling in life. The man was made of methane and had a low and sonorous fart tone that always reminded me of a foghorn sounding out, somewhere far out to sea. The sound of his flatulence gave him a kind of a mysterious appeal that was strangely lost on most of the women we tried to hang around.

"Well I smoked that Labrador Tea just the same," Donny said. "On account of Billy Three-Legs Tootoosis told me I could. I smoked it and then I said I was sorry, because Billy Three-Legs Tootoosis said that you had to apologize to anything that you killed in this life, even if it was only a tea bush."

"Ha," I laughed. "If Billy Three-Legs Tootoosis tells you that shit is ham, are you going to fry yourself up a turd and slide it on in between two slices of fresh buttered bread?"

Billy Three-Legs Tootoosis was our town's resident Indian. It was an honorary position and Billy took it as seriously as if it were something big like the Nobel Peace Prize or the Stanley Cup. People would point at him and make jokes about him. He was kind of upholding a tradition representing the kind of backwoods stereotype that let folks imagine that things didn't really ever need to change.

"Who else would they tell their racist jokes about?" Billy Three-Legs Tootoosis had asked me once after I'd asked him if being the town Indian bothered him any. "I figure I'm taking one for the tribes. So long as I keep grinning and taking it nobody else gets that racist Indian crap dumped on them."

The truth was, most of the real Indians around here preferred to stay on the reservations. They just didn't want to live anywhere close to town on account of the kind of people who lived in towns. Speaking as somebody who lived in town, I figured there was no accounting for taste, I guess.

"Billy Three-Legs Tootoosis is part-Cree," Donny said. "He told me so. He knows a lot about the wilderness and things."

"Billy Three-Legs Tootoosis knows shit," I said. "The closest he ever got to the reservation was all those lonely Saturday nights he spent playing tepee with his wickiup in the back seat of his grandma's Ford pick up truck."

"Do you girls mind shutting up?" Irvin was plainly pissed. "I got something more important on my mind than the fiddling proclivities of Billy Three-Legged's never-to-be-trusted right hand."

Irvin didn't take his eyes off of the trail ahead; he just laid a track out for us to follow, a trail as cold and hard as frozen turds.

"I can still smell that goddamn Hammer Abbey hotel smoke," he said, and we all knew what he was talking about. "And it isn't from any goddamn Labrador tea. I smelled it three goddamn weeks ago and so did you two, if I recollect correctly. And I can still smell it reeking off of that goddamned sad bastard stretched out in our backseat."

"Goddamn, Irvin," I said, trying to lighten the mood. "That's four goddamns in as many sentences. That's got to be some kind of goddamn record. Are you fixing on starting up your own goddamn religion?"

"Why the goddamn hell not?" Irvin asked. "Maybe I will. Call it the High Holy Tracklayers Bullshit-Flinging Church of the One-Eyed Pig-Fuckers complete with clog dancing and free liquor every Saturday night. I reckon it'd beat the hell out of what that old boy upstairs has been dishing out."

It was well said, but I couldn't believe any of what I was hearing. Firstly, I was amazed that Irvin had thought of a name that outdid Trick Magnet H. Flash, but secondly I couldn't believe that somebody could speak so sacrilegiously in the middle of what we were up to.

"Don't tell me you've got a grudge against God?" I said. "Irvin, I know you can get pissy, but how in the hell can you get worked up about somebody we only talk about once a week, excepting hockey season?"

"Just because we don't talk about him, doesn't mean he isn't still hanging over our heads, nosing into our business and butt-fucking our destinies."

"Damn it Irvin," I said. "You could say that about the Prime Minister or the President and you'd be just as right. Why pick on God? He's a good old boy, hung his son on a cross and all that happy puck-shit."

"Do you think so?" Irvin asked. "I've been hearing about how good and kind and merciful that old boy is upstairs, but I've read the Old Testament. You just take a look at all the folks that Jehovah decreed needed to be burned and sacked and smited out of their homes. That old fellow is a psychopathic serial killer, you just check the facts."

"I like cereal ever since I was a kid," Donny said. "Especially the sugary kind, but not Captain Crunch. I like my cereal soggy."

Irvin and I both ignored Donny. Sometimes that boy just insisted on driving in the wrong direction on the wrong side of the road using the Saturday funny pages for a road map.

"Irvin, those are just bible stories," I said. "They don't mean anything."

"They're parables is what they are," Irvin said. "The preacher will read them to you once a week at Sunday school, trying to indoctrinate you into their way of thinking. It's like brainwashing, only dirtier. You got to face up to the facts, Hanny. What happened in the before colors the here and now like permanent oil paint."

"Indoctrinate," I said, going for a grin. "That's a real good word, Irvin. You look that up in your Reader's Digest?"

But Irvin wasn't in a grinning mood. "That's the trouble with you, Hanny. You look at me and all you can see is dumb old Irvin, but I'm a whole lot smarter than you'd think. You can't go on just an appearance. House paint and home improvements don't mean shit."

Here it comes, I thought. Irvin hardly ever said anything, except when he wanted to say a whole lot.

He kept on talking. I figured he'd run out of steam soon enough, but you never could tell with Irvin. Usually he said so very little, that when he started it was kind of like he had to empty out whatever crap he'd been holding back.

"That's the whole problem. Folks are just relying on what they hear about this old fellow God. They look at the pictures and they see this big old Santa Claus-like looking fellow leaning down out of a cloud and cum-showering us with milk and honey and manna-o-manna and they figure he's no worse than Grandpa Walton."

Oh shit. Irvin was getting set to filibuster.

"Well what's so bad about God?" I asked. I knew I was opening a door to a diatribe, but if I didn't open that door he was just going to kick it down all the same and talk all the more. I was his friend. It was part of my job to hear out all of his bullshit, no matter how irritating it got to be. So I let him let it fly, figuring maybe he had a point. Besides, I never did truly trust Will Geer.

Irvin pointed his favourite rude finger straight up at the truck cab's roof.

"I'll tell you what's wrong. Where was that old bastard when this peanut-fart dumped gasoline all over the back room of the Hammer Abbey Railroad Hotel? Where was he when Gil was sucking smoke and chewing on hot cinders? Where was he when the bolts gave way on that rusty old fire escape that should have been replaced back when Christ wore short pants. Where was we when they were hanging out of the windows like fucking Christmas decorations? Where was he and what the fuck was he thinking?"

"Are you done?" I asked.

"Just about," he answered.

With that Irvin bounced the pick-up over a rut that I swore he drove straight through on purpose. I left a Hanny-sized dent in the top of the pick-up can and Tyree bounced hard off of the back seat and wedged down onto the floorboards of the truck. Next thing you know he's jammed down hard and he's making strangled scared noises like he was trying to breathe through the mud-stained upholstery, which I guess he was.

"Fish him up out of there before he chokes to death," Irvin ordered. "Smothering is just too damned easy for this bastard. I want him to pay for what he done, old school Hammurabi-style. An eye for an asshole, fucker. God has spoken."

Donny and I turned around and reached over the ridge of the seat backs to try and haul Tyree up. It was an awkward enough stunt, bellying over the seat backs and reaching down to pick up somebody who didn't want to be picked up. What made it harder was Irvin didn't even bother slowing the truck down.

Tyree didn't help matters any once he started

kicking and bucking like a freshly landed muskellunge.

"Stop that bastard's kicking before he dents up the track cab," Irvin commanded. "I've got one dry nerve left and that rotten eyed prick with ears is pissing all over it."

Right about then a part of me wanted to ask Irvin just when the hell he was going to stop giving us orders and start giving us a hand, but the part of me that stays away from meat run green and dating close cousins decided to shut up for a while and just say nothing. Irvin was a bad man on a good day and tonight was no time to be fucking around.

I reached down for Tyree, but in the dark I was grabbing at the wrong end. He jammed his boots up against my hand, catching all four of my fingers against the side of the truck. I invented a few creative new names for Jesus and all of his saints and a couple of trailer park angels, all the while trying to rise philosophically above the pain.

Which was about the time that Tyree chewed his mouth clear of the duct tape gag we'd wrapped across his lips and sank his dirty uncolgated yellow teeth into the knuckle-hinges of Donny's left hand. Donny let out a noise that sounded a little like Whitney Houston stump-fucking a three year old beagle hound. While Donny was working on the high notes Tyree stomped at my other hand and I sang out in harmony. The Vienna Philharmonic Boys Neutron Choir didn't have a good goddamn thing on us, for sure.

Which was right about the time that we hit the bear.

2

Now the bears around these here parts just aren't that much to speak of. I mean, we're not talking Jeremiah

Johnson can-you-skin-griz grizzly bears here. We're just looking at a bunch of fat old flea-bitten black bears, the welfare bums of the ursine kingdom. You see your average black bear is a whole lot more scared of us humans than we might be scared of them.

Usually.

Part of it comes down to size. If you're looking at a grizzly you're talking about something that can weigh in at over a thousand pounds and stands about ten feet tall, just built for looming and tearing apart whoever happens to be standing before them. Your usual Northern Ontario black bear isn't much bigger than your average St. Bernard. He's built more for rooting around old dead crap, hunting up grubs and garbage and anthills and road kill. They only stand at about four feet tall hunkered down, which is the posture you usually see them in. The black bear's haunches don't allow them much in the way of standing up straight, unless they're pulling themselves up on a tree or a rock or a pick up truck like ours.

That old bear come up over that truck like he was meaning to, hitting face first against the windshield and spraying the glass with a big frothy gust of bear spit and fresh blood. We must have hit the bastard head on. It looked like he'd been running at us, like he figured he could take us down.

Maybe he could.

Irvin stomped on the brakes while his own face was smashing itself up against the windshield glass. For a moment it looked like the two of them, bear and man, were trying to rub themselves cheek to cheek against the hardened glass in a weird kind of Yogi-Bear-Brokeback moment.

I had a pretty good eyeball of the whole sordid proceedings, being flung forward like I was from leaning over the seat back trying to catch hold of Tyree, and then being pitched backwards and lambasting the rear curve of my skull against the dashboard. I remember seeing a cigarette burn mark right beside my right cheekbone, charred into the vinyl of the dash where somebody had crushed out a cigarette. The burn mark looked a little like the shape of Italy, like a boot, you know? At that moment in time it seemed like the most important thing in the world was for me to remember just what sort of shape that cigarette burn looked like.

Donny was lying flat on top of my back, and he was still hanging on to Tyree. Or rather, Tyree was hanging onto Donny's hand with his teeth. The momentum of the collision had hauled Tyree up from under the seat. He wiggled himself up over the seat backs, moving pretty spry for a fellow bound with rope and wire and duct tape. Then he caterpillar-humped his way up over Donny and me, planted his boots against the angle of the front seat and sprung-kicked himself straight out through the already bear-broken windshield.

I don't quite know where he figured he was going to get to, launching himself that way, but it was a pretty goddamned impressive sight I've got to tell you. We're talking scud missiles and catapulting burning bushes. He went up through that windshield glass like he was part Evel Knievel and part John Shaft. Mind you, the bear had weakened the window considerably.

"Get hold of that hot fingered, light footed asshole," Irvin shouted, trying to haul himself free from his seat belt. By now Irvin's face was war-painted with his own blood and at that particular moment he looked a whole lot more native than Billy Three-Legs Tootoosis could have hoped to look like following a month of Indian sunburns and Tonto freestyle rap lessons.

I reached out my arm like a JC Pentecostal on the cross, and wrapped my stoved-up fingers around the door handle. Then I jacked the handle up and felt the mechanism unlatch, but with Donny still spread-eagled across my backbone, I couldn't do much more than hold the door open just wide enough to let a few more bloodthirsty Northern Ontario mosquitoes into the truck cab to feed upon our freshly spilled vitality.

Next thing I knew I felt Donny's boots going up and over my backbone like it was a stepladder, and he's going right up over the bear's head, trying to catch hold of our runaway arsonist.

I had to give the boy credit. He might have been a few beers short of a six-pack, but he was never much backward when it comes to going straight forward. If something needed doing, Donny wasn't shy about holding back. He was up and at it, ready for whatever come his way.

At least that's how Donny looked to be feeling until the bear woke back up.

3

It was enough to piss off the Good Humour man.

Here we were set out to build ourselves a little home-made revenge when God or Mother Nature decided to deal themselves in for a hand or two and fuck our expectations up like a herd of horny track men racing into a whorehouse on a Sudbury Saturday night.

Donny had one boot on the top of my shoulder blade and the other planted on the hood of the truck, looking for all the world like a reluctant surfer stepping up to ride the curl of a particularly dangerous wave, staring face-first into the muzzle of a pissed-off truck-slammed five hundred pound black bear.

I pushed on the door and rolled out of the truck like I thought I was in the middle of a Miami Vice episode. I don't rightly know what the hell I thought I was going to do, but all that I knew was I had to do it fast.

I couldn't see what Irvin was up to. Tyree was on the ground at the bear's feet, making a determined rolling wiggle towards the road. I wasn't worried about him. I was worried about Donny, who was just about to get his fool head chewed off.

I stepped up and shoved my hand, the same damn hand that Tyree had already stomped the hell out of, straight into the face of the bear, accidentally jamming my thumb into its eye socket. It didn't seem to see me coming, especially once my thumb was in its eye. It might have been that it was busy reaching out for Donny. It might be that the bear's peripheral vision had been somewhat fucked up by the collision with the truck. The possibilities were damn near endless but the amount of time in which I had to consider my options was pretty fucking nearly infinitesimal.

I leaned forward and jammed my thumb deeper into the bear's left eye, chocked my boot heel against the truck's front tire and braced myself hard, like I figured I was going to hold this bear at bay all by myself.

There's only one way to say this. A bear's head is freaking goddamn big. Even a Northern Ontario black bear can be a hell of a handful once you are stupid enough to get your hands wrapped around him. I could feel the bones in the black bear's face moving like fur-covered plate armour beneath my splayed open hand. So far I wasn't doing anything much more useful than pissing old Yogi off.

This one-handed Horatio-at-the-bridge Mexican bear stand-off had to be the one of the stupidest tricks I'd ever tried, and you have to keep in mind that this was coming from the fellow who once had roller skated through his high school prom with nothing on but a pair of Tinkerbelle wings and a camouflage of peppermint flavoured body paint. In about the time it took me to stick my thumb in and wiggle it around in the jelly-meat, I was certain that old bear was going to whirl about and rip my arm off and feed it back to me one knuckle at a time.

Bluntly put, I was fucked.

Only instead of ripping my arm off the bear stopped stock still and uttered out a roar that made Donny's Whitney Houston beagle call sound like a popcorn fart in the middle of a machine gun shoot-out in a Chinese gong factory. Mentioning a thunderstorm right about now would be just guilding the lily.

"Get the hell," I started to say, trying to yell at Donny to get the hell out of here, half expecting that big bruin bastard to toothpick my arm bone down to splintery forget-me-knuckles, when all of a sudden Irvin stepped up out of nowhere, quicker than you could say shit skidded skivvies, and slammed the business end of a genuine German Luger smack-square-dab into the side of the bear's skull and fired three shots off fast.

"Shit!"

I stepped back too slow, my thumb still jammed into the bear's left eye socket. My ears were ringing the Hallelujah Chorus with a Jimmy Page background of Hendrix-inspired guitar riffs. The side of my face was covered with what felt like bear brains. There were probably bits of the big old bastard's skull mixed in there with the shot-out bear brains, but I couldn't tell for sure. The whole world was ringing way too goddamn fast.

For a moment all I could do was stand there and stare at the bear's blown-out skull. The side of it was open wide enough for a red-headed woodpecker to build himself a comfortable nest. And then the damndest thing happened. I stood there staring and it looked like the bear was talking to me.

"Cover your tracks," the dead bear said. "Where ever you been ain't necessarily where ever you're going," Which at the time made about as much sense as a talking dead bear did.

"Only you can prevent forest fires," I answered back in a blurry bear-wrestling truck-wrecked brain-spattered kind of a daze.

Then I shook my head and looked again and the bear was deader than the disco duck and everything appeared natural. We were three guys and one convicted and duct taped arsonist, standing in the heart of the Northern Ontario woods over the body of a dead black bear. I expected we made an interesting tableau.

"Let go of that bear and stop messing around," Irvin said.

"Jesus Christ," I swore, dragging my hand clear of the poked-out eye socket. "You could have blown my hand off."

"I think I did," Irvin said.

I looked down at the hand.

Shit. He had. My thumb was half-missing. I could see a bit of the bone poked out like the stump of a broken pencil stub. The rest of the thumb looked like it had been run through an electronic pencil sharpener.

I tried to pinch the wound off, hoping to stop the bleeding, but I might as well try to stop traffic with a dirty look. Little spurts of blood shot out from the blasted thumb end. It felt like I was jerking off my thumb. I hope it respected me in the morning.

"Here," Irvin said, tearing a chunk from his t-shirt. "Wrap it in this."

"You shot my goddamn thumb off Irvin." I said while wrapping it in the t-shirt tear-off, trying hard not to wonder when the last time Irvin had washed this particular shirt was.

"You'll be okay," he told me.

"You shot my goddamned thumb off," I repeated. It was important to keep the facts straight.

"That's one less nail you'll have to clip," he offered.

"Think of the money you'll save in manicures."

"It's my fucking thumb." I was losing it, and it was no wonder. You can hold an awful lot of pain in one hand, and nearly twice as much in one finger. That's how come hangnails hurt so badly.

"The bear would have done a whole lot worse," Irvin noted.

He had a point. I tried to grin around it, but the whiz-bang was wearing off, and I was starting to feel my thumb throbbing.

"Fuck," I said, scared and impressed at the same damned time. "We did it. You and I, we killed a bear with our bare hands."

"We didn't do it alone," Irvin said, pointing down at the dirt. "We did have ourselves a bit of help."

I looked down. There on the ground were Donny and Tyree. Tyree, bound hands and all, had both of his fists wrung white-knuckled around the bear's nuts, like a kid hanging onto a trick or treat bag. I figured that must have been what had distracted the bear just long enough for Irvin to get in there and administer his fistful of Luger lobotomy.

"Where the hell did that gun come from, anyway?" I asked.

"It was a World War 2 souvenir taken right off of an SS Hauptsturmfuhrer," Irvin said. "It was a gift from my grandfather. He brought it home from the war, along with a case of penicillin-resistant Belgian clap and a dirty French tattoo that looked a little like a turtle having sex with the pyramids of the Nile. I figured it might be handy to have along with me tonight, given the sort of work we were up to."

"Shit," I said. "All I got from my grandpa was this stupid assed name."

"Never mind the sorry state of your birthright," Irvin said. "Stop your yakking and get Donny the hell out of there."

That's when I looked down at Donny for the first time since Irvin had simultaneously shot the bear and my thumb off.

What the fuck?

It was around then that the bear brains that were splattered on the side of my skull started to itch as if they were crawling for my cowlick. It felt like they were trying to tell me something, but I didn't pay them any mind. I was stuck there, stock still, staring down at Donny. At first glance it looked like Donny was nuzzling the bear's tail, like he was trying to make a telephone call straight up through the bear's asshole.

Then I looked closer.

Donny's arm was jammed nearly elbow deep up the bear's tailpipe. He must have round-housed it in there fist first. I had to wonder at the nerve it must have took, dry-fisting a goddamn black bear square in the middle of a moonless night halfway through a one-handed shoot-out.

"That's who the hell you can thank for saving your life," Irvin pointed out.

"Holy crap," I said.

"And then some," Irvin said.

Donny just laid there, his face as white as a bucket of washed over bleach, making fresh-caught trout faces with his mouth.

It was as delicate a situation as trying to extract a bushel of live cats from out of a bucket of dead porcupines. I reached my good hand down and caught hold of Donny's arm and helped him up from the dirt, while Irvin just stood there and snickered. I guess having a loaded pistol in your belt gave a fellow a certain sense of authority.

Donny's other arm came out of the bear's poop chute, with a cheek-flapping wet-fart sound. Donny's arm was covered in blood and some of the blackest and foulest crap I'd ever seen. It didn't smell one bit like lilies of the valley.

"Jesus Christ, Donny," I said. "You must have had your arm worked right up into that there bear's lower colon."

Donny made a few more fish faces. He was shivering in spite of the fact that it was August-hot and sticky out here.

"Get up here, Donny," I said, leaning back and putting my weight into it. He stood shakily, like a house of cards just waiting to be blown down. He held his poop stained arm off to one side, like he might have wanted to yank it out of its socket and throw it away on the compost heap. All the same, he was hanging onto something that might have been a piece of bear crap, or maybe the bear's pancreas.

"I got it," Donny said. He was still shaking, his bones poured from rubber earthquakes and slinky wire.

"What do you got Donny?" I asked slowly.

Donny looked up at me just as slowly, like he'd just done the single biggest thing in the world, and I guess he had.

"I got hold of the bear's soul," he said, holding the fistful out towards me.

I didn't want to look at whatever he was holding. It was small and it seemed to be moving.

"It's his soul," Donny said. "As long as I got it he ain't going anywhere."

Having woken up in my share of ugly married women's beds I knew damn well what shock could do to a man, so I phrased my next words carefully.

"You did good Donny," I told him.

"I ain't letting go," he said, pushing the piece of bear at my face.

I made a few fresh-caught trout mouths of my own, and then he smiled that Donny smile of his again and I figured everything was going to be okay, sooner or later.

"I'm holding it tight," Donny said. "There's got to be some kind of sacrifice."

He wasn't making much sense, but how much sense could I expect after what we'd been through. I decided that he'd be okay, although I wasn't all that sure about myself.

"We got to eat it," Donny said.

"Huh?"

"We got to eat the bear," Donny said. "You can't kill something wild for no reason. It's a sin."

I was about to point out that self-preservation counts high among my reasons for bear slaughter, when Irvin spoke up.

"He's right," Irvin said. "We got to eat some of it."

He knelt down with his hunting knife in his hands, already hacking into the hide and cutting loose a chunk of meat. "We don't have to eat it all. Just a bit will do."

"Irvin, are you completely fucked in the head, or just generally soft?"

Irvin stared at me, his eyes as hard and deep as the twin barrels of a shotgun.

"We got to eat some of the meat," he repeated. "And then we got to apologise for killing it. Billy Three-Legs Tootoosis is a hell of a lot smarter than he looks."

He threw me his Zippo.

"Start a fire," he said. "But careful, mind you, we don't want to be setting the whole damned place ablaze."

4

Well I wouldn't exactly call it hot cuisine. The fact was it wasn't even close to tepid. We didn't have enough time to build a bed of coals, so we settled for charring it over the open flames. We held it off to one side so that the bear fat wouldn't flare up in the flames, turning it rotisserie style to keep the juices from running off of it and drying it out. I'm certain we picked up enough pestilence and corruption to single-handedly bring about the rebirth of the Bubonic Plague, but we got her down and said our apologies and made things right with the Great Spirit or whoever the hell was watching from up there above the pines.

"Well that hit the spot," Irvin said.

"Would that be the spot of indigestion or that spot of pneumatic botulism that is germinating somewhere southwest of my lower intestine?" I asked.

"Quit your belly aching," Irvin chided me. "Let's get this asshole under way."

He pointed at Tyree.

Only I got to wondering about Tyree. The fact was, I'd be wondering all of the way through the bear meat. What Tyree had done hadn't been all that much compared to arm-fucking a full grown black bear, but who was to say that bear hadn't been held back just enough on account of Tyree hanging on so tightly to Fozzie's funky fuzzy teabags. Who was to say that Tyree hadn't just saved my life, as much as Irvin kept telling me it was Donny who'd done the deed?

"Get that thought out of your head right now," Irvin warned me like he could read my mind. "He didn't save you. Donny did."

I stared at Irvin. He always had a touch of magic and secrecy about him, what with his making guns appear and seeing in the dark and knowing the proper apologies to make to a dead bear. All the same, I had to argue with him this time.

"Are you sure about that?" I asked.

"I said it, didn't I?"

Irvin wasn't known for much exaggeration. The man had all of the imagination of petrified dog turd.

"So what's your verdict, your honour?" I asked, pointing down at Tyree. "What the hell do you figure we ought to do with him for now?"

Irvin looked over at me as if I'd just said the stupidest thing since tri-party politics.

"What the fuck else do you figure we're going to do?" Irvin said. "The same thing we came out here to do in the first place."

Irvin hawked up a jumbo-sized loogie and let it gravitationally anoint itself down onto the top of Tyree's head. It hit home with a soft wet plop that sounded like it would stay stuck for a hell of a long time.

"We're going to kill the little fucker, that's what we're going to do."

5

We darked the lights on the truck and left it where it was, hoping that the engine would start when we got back. We'd borrowed the truck from the freight yard, and would have to get it back by morning, but if we had to leave it here we'd probably be safe enough. These trucks went missing all the time, and like it as not they'd just blame it on Tyree and call it a day.

"What the hell kind of name is Tyree, anyway?" Irvin asked.

"How the fuck should I know?" I asked. "Maybe he made it up."

"Who in the hell would make up their own name?"

I was thinking about my own name, and how I planned to change it.

"A lot of people change their names," I said. "Folks are re-inventing themselves all of the time."

"Don't fix nothing if it isn't broke," Irvin said.

"What do you think, Donny?"

"I wonder if there are any more bears out here." Donny wondered aloud.

It was a good question, given all that had happened.

"If there is any more out there Donny, you can syrup them up with your sweet talking before up and fist-fucking them to death," Irvin said.

I glowered at Irvin's back. The man had all the sensitivity of a sandblast enema.

"There ain't nothing out here but trees and rocks and the dark, and a whole lot of fucking mosquitoes," I said, trying to cheer Donny up.

"What's over them hills, do you figure?" he asked.

"More hills," Irvin said. "Let's get moving."

We followed the railroad tracks, straight on out into the darkness of the night. I did my best to stay downwind of Donny. The bear stink on him was beginning to fulminate. We both were stinking of bear, shit, fear and genuine funk. I heard there were folks in Korea who would pay an awful lot for a bear's gall bladder. I figured between what Donny was wearing on his arm and the halo of minced bear head cheese I was wearing on my forehead we ought to have both been worth a small fortune on eBay.

We kept on walking, one step after another.

About that time the bear brains started talking to me, good and loud.

6

Now talking is a good thing. It's how we fill in the gaps between what needs doing, what wants doing, and whatever the hell we're dreaming about doing when we stare up at the ceiling before falling into sleep. Talk is a kind of glue that holds lives together. It's not the work that you do that makes the engineer such a good buddy to the guy working in the caboose. It's the stories that you tell over a beer or a coffee or a campfire that makes a man's memories loom out loud and long.

So maybe that's what this bear was doing, trying to talk to me. Maybe he was trying to get to know what it was like to have thumbs and worry about something else besides making a few more cubs and fattening that belly that needed filling by winter. Maybe he was just trying to understand the simple asshole that had left the tip of his thumb buried in the humorous jelly of his left eye socket, just an inch or two shy of his Jasper-Jellystone dreaming frontal lobe.

Or maybe he was just fucking around in whatever roomy dark cave of an afterlife Northern Ontario black bears inhabit after they been Lugered to death.

"The path is long," the spirit of the bear said to me. "And it touches all sides."

"No kidding," I said. "You ought to try walking it while you're dragging a duct taped arsonist in tow."

"Whiner," the dead bear said.

"Winnie," I retorted.

Repartee is my middle name. You get a lot of practise up here in Northern Ontario, in between the crib and the curling and listening to the diesels hoot down the line. Life up here has its own kind of rhythm, hard and driving like a train engine, and then there's them long stretches of quiet in between, and it hardly surprises a fellow when he can find himself the time to converse with the dead spirit of a black bear.

"Should I apologise again?" I asked. "I know the Cree are big about apologising to the animals they catch and kill. It wasn't really me that killed you. You know that, don't you? I'm just the guy who fondled your left eye socket up close and personal. In some cultures that's often considered a kind of pre-emptive mating strike."

"That's okay," the spirit of the bear said. "Shit happens, every day. It all gets washed away in the flush of life."

"Hakuna Matata," I agreed. "What goes around comes around."

"The past is nothing more than a canvas for what's going on right now," the bear expounded. The spirit of the bear was making a surprising amount of sense, given that he was dead and all. Maybe that gave him a little sense of perspective.

"Dead men walk the tracks," the dead bear said.

I looked over at the rails, and all at once I could see the spirits of the dead men walking, the navvies and the chinks and the road gangs who'd laid down the steel and the timber like a stitch sewn out across a giant forever carcass.

"But they tell no tales," I answered.

"They tell no tales but they sure as hell leave trails," the dead bear said.

"You're bound and determined to get the last word in, ain't you?" I said.

In the chat-room of my inner child imagination I stared into the dead bear's eyes. They seemed like black holes, sucking me downward. I could see something swimming up towards me in the dark sea of the dead bear's eyes. It looked a little like Irvin.

"Earth to Hanny, Earth to Hanny, Houston we have got a fucking problem."

"Huh?" I looked around. The bear was gone. Irvin was staring at me like I was a bug under a microscope. Only something was changed. Irvin was wearing a robe of bear fur and black feathers that looked like it might have been growing out of his skin.

"You were sleepwalking," he said. "And talking to your self."

"Daydreaming, I guess," I said.

"Not dreaming," Irvin corrected. "You've been walking wide. That's a danger in the dark places of the North woods. There are shadows out here cast by no tree or rock. Dark places where you can step through into another plane of existence."

I looked up at Irvin, and I could see it wasn't really Irvin.

"I must still be dreaming," I said. "You're Irvin, only not Irvin."

"Not dreaming. You've been walking wide. There's a big difference," Irvin-not-Irvin said. "The world used to be a dark colorless plain of nothingness. There weren't any people or plants or animals. There weren't any mountains, lakes or forests. There was nothing but nothingness. Then the spirit awoke from the shadows and stood up and began rooting around in the darkness looking for food or drink. He turned up mountains, and pissed down rivers, and the dreams he planted grew up into people and animals and birds and life. Then they all started moving around in the darkness, stirring up the wind and calling down the rain and drawing out the moon, and the fire that burned in their collective hearts grew out to become the sun."

"I have no fucking idea what you are talking about," I said to Irvin-not-Irvin.

Irvin-not-Irvin smiled. His smile looked a little like Donny's, crooked at one side like his happiness was leaking out.

"Sure you do," Irvin-not-Irvin said. "We all know it when we go dreaming, when we go walking wide. We're all part of this world and when we touch it there are ripples that sing out and touch everything else. Man, woman, moose and bear. We're all a part of this big wide walking, reaching out in every direction, touching everywhere and everything all at once."

Then Irvin-not-Irvin winked, and in his wink I saw the great one-eyed bear, with my own thumbprint still burning somewhere deep inside that black hole eye socket.

Irvin-not-Irvin smiled one more time, that half-cracked Donny smile of his that he'd borrowed or maybe owned in the first place.

"Wake up," Irvin-not-Irvin said, and I did.

7

"Shit," I said, starting my eyes open.

"Wake up," Irvin said. "You're asleep at the switch and we got work to do."

"Shit, shit," I repeated.

"You're covered in it. So is Donny. That happens sometimes. We still got work to do. Stop talking to yourself and let's get to it."

I hadn't been talking to myself, and I knew that for a fact, but I wasn't about to argue the point with Irvin.

"Sorry," I said, because it seemed simpler than trying to explain what I'd just been through. Simpler, on account of I wasn't all that sure myself what I'd just been through.

"I'm awake now Irvin," I assured him.

He grunted, like he wasn't all that certain if I was or not.

"You've been talking to the bear, haven't you?" Irvin asked.

I looked back at Irvin, double checking to make sure I wasn't still dreaming.

"How the fuck did you know?" I asked him.

"Who else is out here to talk to?" Irvin said, like it made all of the sense in the world. "Now come on. It's been a long night, but we've still got a long way to go."

It turned out to be a whole lot longer than the three of us could have ever guessed.

8

We were about five miles out from town and my feet were channelling the bunions of the collective casualties of the Trail of Tears and the Bataan Death March. We were far enough down the line that it wasn't likely there'd be any switchman humping boxcars down this way and accidentally disturbing us before we were finished.

Finished. That was one hell of a word. How do you tie up a knot like this one? I knew where this was all going to end but I don't know how in hell we ever figured it was going to be anywhere close to be being finished.

"Do we have to do this?" I asked Irvin.

"What kind of a question is that?" Irvin asked back. "The bastard burned a couple of your buddies to death and killed my big brother. He sent them up in flames like last year's gas bill. What the hell else can we do?"

"You're sure about that are you?" Tyree asked. "You figure I did all that you think I did?"

We all jumped like flung-bungeed cats. These were the first words Tyree had said all night, since we'd jumped him outside of the Legion Hall and tied him up and gagged him. He hadn't even said anything after he'd chewed the duct tape gag loose. Maybe he figured on saving his breath for his death song.

Personally, I didn't understand this kind of thinking. If I was walking my last mile and knew it, I don't believe I'd shut up for a minute. I'd talk a steel blue streak, trying to make up for everything I wasn't going to be able to say later. There are a whole lot of things I haven't had a chance to say yet.

Then there were all of those things I missed the chance to say. Things that I wished I had the chance to say, even now. I wished I could go back and tell Beth Skinner how hot she had looked in her cinnamon and lemonade striped cheerleading outfit, back before Marie and I said "I do" to each other. I wished I had told my high school track instructor what a colossal aneurism he'd been for taking me off of the track team just as I was getting fast enough to break the school record in the 100 yard dash just because I'd gone and chucked our champion javelin chucker straight through three lockers full of soccer balls, for having the nerve to look sideways at my girlfriend's ass. I wished I'd had the chance to tell the javelin chucker how sorry I was that there hadn't been a fourth locker.

And more than anything I wished that I'd found the time to tell my dad how much I looked up to him, back before I found myself staring down at him laying there in that long dark box.

If I closed my eyes now I knew I would see him staring up at me out of the darkness, his face as cold and hard as that last chunk of frozen purple meat at the bottom of the deep freeze. I knew he would open his mouth and he would say something to me in the voice of the bear that I just didn't think I wanted to hear right now.

So I kept my eyes open and promised myself I wouldn't blink.

"I think we ought to let him talk," I said.

"Who, Donny?"

"No, Tyree."

"What for?" Irvin asked. "Just a waste of good air, if you ask me. Haven't you heard there's an ozone crisis going on? Keep yakking like you are, using up all of that good atmosphere, and we're all going to need to wipe our assholes with SPF 75 sunscreen."

"Donny's bean-farts do just as much damage to the

ozone layer," I pointed out. "Besides, I think Tyree deserves a say in this."

"He's had his say. He said it when the first flames went up. He said it when my brother's face started to split open from the heat, all sizzling like bear meat grilling down on the barbecue."

"I think Hanny is right," Donny said. "We all ought to have a say."

"Sure you all ought to," Irvin said. He whirled back around, back-handing Donny so hard that one of his teeth spit out. "What do you have to say to that, fuckhead?"

Donny hit the ground. His mouth was bleeding.

"I think he chipped my toof," Donny said.

He tried to grin, but it was all lopsided and wrong. That Donny smile didn't quite look the same. Something had been twisted in it and I didn't think it could ever be fixed.

I looked at Irvin, hard as I could.

"You didn't have to do that Irvin," I said.

"Didn't not have to do it either," Irvin said right back at me. "Now shut the fuck up. We're here."

Sure enough we were, right at Five mile switch, out amongst the tall jack pines. You could see the signs of the old bushfire if you knew what to look for. It had taken out the woods for miles. Everybody figured it for a heat lightning strike. Donny and I had been out here blueberry picking. We caught shit for wandering so damn far off the track.

Now there was nothing but jack pines and more blueberries. The pines always came back after the fire rolled through. There was something in the heat that popped their seeds from the pine cones. The blueberries grew thicker than usual here as well. I guess ashes were great for fertilizer.

There was nothing else out here, but the switch.

And us.

Irvin looked down at his glow-in-the-dark wristwatch.

"We got eight minutes," he said. "Let's get to it."

I did my best to let Tyree down gently onto the track, but Irvin shoved me and him down as hard as he could.

"Asshole," Irvin said. "You fellows couldn't tie your shoes together without a detailed set of paint-by-number instructions. Stop dicking around and get his hand jammed down into that switch."

A railroad switch is a pretty simple device, designed to join two ends of track together, when a train is leaving one track and traveling onto another. Basically, there's a big swing bar of steel that levers back and forth. The train follows the swing bar, either straight on, or onto another track. There's a gap in between the swing bar and the rail that closes tight when the swing bar moves. A fellow had best be careful about where he sets his boot when he's crossing the tracks. If he gets his foot jammed in a swinging switch, he's apt to bust an ankle, or worse.

"This is sure going to hurt," Donny said.

"No worse than proctologically poking your arm up a bear's butt," Irvin pointed out. "This bastard deserves it."

Donny and I just stared at each other. We'd been beat and broken and damn near bear-bitten. The fact was we were just too tired and broke down to argue the point. We'd do whatever Irvin told us to.

Soldiers get that way in battle. The sergeant says get up over that hill and face down the machine gun, and up over the hill they go. It works the same way on section gangs and track crews. Whatever the foreman says, sooner or later goes.

Donny and I forced Tyree's left hand down into the switch, between the swinging bar and the rail. The switch was set electronically and a computer timing device three hundred miles away would shift the switch over, bringing the two pieces of metal together, so that the CPR train could successfully switch onto the CNR track.

By Irvin's watch this entire process would take place in about six minutes time.

Tyree tried to kick free, but the two of us had a firm grip on him now. There didn't seem to be much fight left in him. I guess he was tired too.

"Tyree," Irvin said. "You've been found guilty of setting a match and gasoline to the Hammer Abbey Railroad Hotel and smoking six men to death, as well as Henry Tompkins, the night clerk, and a perfectly good tomcat named One-Eye. One of those men was my brother, Gilbert. For burning him and those six other fellows, you're going to have to die."

Tyree just lay there and stared up at the three of us. That made it worse. It might have been easy if he'd kept on fighting. That would have given us something to do while we were holding his hand down, waiting for the switch to swing shut.

"You got anything to say in your defence?"

"What the fuck good would it do if I did?" Tyree asked. "I've got nothing to say that you want to hear."

"Irvin, I don't think he did it," Donny said.

"What?" Irvin asked.

"I said I don't think he did it."

Irvin stared at Donny. I could feel the strength of his gaze even in the darkness, shining out at us like the blind beam of a flashlight.

"You got something to say?"

"I don't think he did it," Donny repeated for the third time.

"Donny, I truly like you," Irvin said. "You're a good boy, and there's damn few men would have jammed their arm where you did, but sometimes you act dumb enough to dig fence postholes in a snow bank."

Donny opened his mouth to speak, and the switch closed shut. I was holding Tyree's arm at the wrist when the steel closed. I felt the chill of the cold steel rail kiss the side of my pinkie and the sensation damn near leaped up and burned me. It didn't make much of a noise coming together on Tyree's hand, just a sort of a crackling quiet like someone crumpling up a potato chip bag in the dark.

Tyree yelled loud enough to out-deafen those three bear-killing Luger shots and Donny's beagle-humping Whitney Houston serenade. He screamed all of the breath out of his lungs, and a few molecules of oxygen that he'd sucked in from his mama's umbilical, back when he was floating around in her belly-tank. The scream lasted a good minute, and then bled off to a rasping sort of sigh. All the color left Tyree's face and ran out onto the dirt of the trackside. I could see Tyree's face pale and glowing, like he'd grown a moon atop his shoulders and then everything went calm.

Tyree lay there staring up at me. I wondered if he was bleeding or if maybe the switch had closed tightly enough to cut off his arterial flow. I wondered about the band-aid qualities of a CNR rail, not having much faith in a cauterization by steel. I had the feeling that maybe the metal was drinking Tyree's blood. I could picture that, the blood flowing through the steel rail, like a fat rusty vein running right across this continent. All of the men who'd given their lives to building this rail line, one dead man for every foot of steel some folks said, their blood was still pumping in the piston of the diesel and the scream of the train.

I saw the bear looking one-eyed out from both of Tyree's eyes. It was trying to tell me something and for the life of me I couldn't understand what.

"He's as guilty as Iscariott," Irvin pronounced. "And now he's fucked."

Irvin looked down at his wristwatch. I saw his face

shining in the soft electronic glow.

"How much time?" I asked.

"That train will be here in five minutes," Irvin said. "The switch will hold him fast enough until the train rolls out the guilt in him. When that comes we'd best make ourselves scarce."

I stood up, half expecting Tyree to start kicking, but all of the fight had gone out of him. He lay there on the tracks with his left hand vanished between those two bars of iron rail like it had been cut clean off. He kind of looked a little like Donny, with his arm jammed inside the bear's pooper.

"The train'll roll over him, the switch'll click back, and they'll think he was out here drinking." Irvin said. "Some folks will say accident and others will whisper suicide and everybody will privately figure that Tyree finally got just what was coming to him.

"What if they CSI his body?" Donny asked. "We got our fingerprints all over him."

"You watch too damn much television," Irvin said. "This is the town police we're talking about. On the first account there won't be any body left, once that train rolls over it. They'll be picking Tyree up in a bushel basket, assuming the bears and raccoons and crows don't get him, assuming there are any bears left after Daniel bear-fucker Boone here gets done with fist-fucking them all to death."

Irvin kept on hammering on that bear-fucking crack. I figured it had to hurt, but Donny didn't say anything. He just stood there, hanging onto whatever he'd dragged out of that bear, looking down at Tyree.

I placed the sole of my boot flat out onto the rail. I felt the vibration of the distant train, humming through the steel. It was coming soon.

"Can you feel it coming?" Irvin asked.

I nodded.

Tyree just lay there.

"Right on time," Irvin nodded. He was pleased with how it was all going down, like he'd finished a job on schedule.

"Irvin," Donny said. "He didn't do it."

"What?"

"I'm telling you he didn't do it."

I could hear the train in the distance now. I could hear something even stronger in Donny's voice.

"How do you know he didn't?" Irvin asked, laying his words out slow.

"I just know."

I could see the light in the distance, the headlamp shining out like a long bright knife into the wooded darkness. I bet you God sees the world that way, with one good eye staring out into the lying shadows.

"I just know," Donny repeated, and that's all I let him get out. The train was close enough to see us, if we didn't move fast.

"Jump," I shouted, catching the two of them by their necks and pushing us all three down into the darkness of the surrounding bushes as the train rolled on by.

We lay there in the darkness listen to the chunk-chunk-chunk as the cars rolled over the track.

"Stay down," I whispered to Donny.

Right about then I was telling him a whole lot more than just stay down in the dirt. I was begging him to keep whatever he wanted to say to himself. We'd just killed Tyree. He needed to die, on account of Irvin said so. I couldn't live with any other kind of reality, right now.

That train was coming fast. I could hear it in the distance, even smell it coming, singing out in the hum of the steel rail, and the chunking sound as it rolled over each hard-buried iron spike. I heard the roar of the bear mauling through the thunder of the diesel and the steel.

And then it was on us. The train rolled and roared past, and then it was thunder all around us, the steady chunk-chunk-chunk sound as each truck wheel rolled over the properly closed switch.

I thought about Tyree, under those wheels. There was no way he could have escaped. I wondered how long he'd feel the steel rolling across each nerve. How long does a memory scream?

I pictured him caught up underneath the steel wheels, dragged and broken and torn and flung. I kept expecting to hear a scream. I don't know how I'd figure I'd hear it over the hungry roar of the train. Death would travel far faster than any scream could ever hope to run. Tyree's throat would be torn out and pulped, and the memory of last night's song in the shower and the "Get fucked," he'd thrown at a co-worker and the half-assed joke he'd cracked to the cute Tim Horton's waitress would all be flattened out onto the steel rails, to couple with the lonely working dreams of all of the navvies and the chinks and the working men who had died laying these tracks down across our wide impassive country over the last century, making a scar that wouldn't stick.

If a scream had worked its way up through Tyree's trachea and harped through the plucking vocal chords it would have been whisked away in the slipstream of the rushing steel wheels.

I couldn't deal with that thought. I pushed my face down into the dirt and the dead pine needles, smelling the ash of the long forgotten bushfire hiding deep in the dirt, a last track and trace of that long ago fire and in the silence of the roaring steel tracks behind me I heard Donny saying over and over to Irvin, "He didn't do it, he didn't do it," in tune with the song of the rail and I wondered who did.

There was only one way to find out.

I rolled over and I caught Donny in a neck hold. I had grown up watching Jean Carpentier and Killer Kowalski and Mad Dog Vachon going at it in the Grand Prix wrestling ring. I knew the flying mare and the arm bar and the incapacitating eye gouge. I could even fake a pretty good drop kick, although it usually resulted in inflicting more injury upon me than upon the inflictee.

The only problem with this reasoning was that Donny had watched all of those matches with me, and he knew just as many tricks. He eeled out of my neck hold and pistoned an elbow back into the side of my head. I felt that elbow greasing off of the bear brains, and I wondered if the black bear's brains would have anything to say to Donny's elbow bone.

We rolled up against the roots of a jack pine and Donny pulled loose and kicked back at me. I felt Donny's mule-kicking work boots working over my ribs, and I reached up blindly past his boot and followed the trail of denim up to the crotch. I caught hold of what counted and I squeezed.

Tyree had taught me a trick or two, too.

Donny howled like a gut shot wolf, making a face that only a necrophiliac could love, sucking in his cheeks and owling out his eyes and rolling them back until I was certain he was staring directly at his long lost childhood memories. I kept on squeezing, going for broke.

"Who did it, Donny?" I asked, hanging onto his denimed testicles. "Who burned the hotel down?"

"I didn't mean to," Donny said, weeping real tears. "I didn't mean to start the fire."

"*What?*" I asked.

He was crying, the snot rolling and slithering out of his nose, the sobs hitching along like boxcars loaded full of guilt.

"I didn't mean to start the fire," Donny repeated.

And then Irvin was on him, throwing me aside like I was a discarded beer can, catching hold of Donny by the throat and shaking him like he expected a money back refund.

"What'd you say?" Irvin asked. "What the fuck did

you say?"

Donny was back to making those trout faces again. Irvin kept throttling and shaking him, not letting up for a minute, looking for an answer but not letting one escape.

"What'd you say?" Irvin repeated.

I tried to catch hold of Irvin and pull him off of Donny, but I would have had better luck trying to pull an unshot-up black bear from off of a honey-packed beehive. Irvin was tensed steel, shot through with a white hot line of blue lightning, strung with hatred and an undeniable need for vengeance.

"What the fuck did you say?"

By now his voice was so hoarse I could hear the bear growling in his throat, like it had climbed down inside of him and taken over his existence.

Donny didn't stand a chance. Irvin had his hands around Donny's throat and was squeezing the breath out of him. It takes a lot to kill a man by bare-handed strangulation. It isn't as easy as they show on the television. There's muscle in your neck and your shoulders, especially when you've worked for a living like we had.

Still, Donny wasn't looking that good. Irvin was pretty determined to get his fair share of mayhem in. If assault and battery were a pinball game Irvin had just racked up a score that tallied way past the free game mark.

I tried wrapping my arms around Irvin's waist, hoping to bear-hug him away from Donny. That didn't work nearly as well as it did on television either. Big John of the roller derby Thunderbirds always made it look damn easy, but I might as well have been trying to throttle an oak tree.

"Irvin," I tried shouting at him. "He didn't fucking do it, Irvin."

But Irvin wasn't listening.

I kept reaching around, and then I felt the butt of the

Luger. I drew it out of Irvin's belt and jammed it into his ear canal as hard as I could.

"If you don't let go of him, Irvin," I said, shouting loud enough for him to hear me through the pistol barrel. "I'm going to have to blow your skull out."

I didn't know how to cock the fucking gun, so I settled for making a click sound with my tongue and teeth, hoping I sounded dangerous.

He seemed to hear that click loud and clear or maybe the barrel was talking through the grip of my fist.

I'd never fired a Luger before. I'd only seen them in World War II movies. I hadn't fired any hand guns at all, now that I thought of it. The closest I'd come was my six-shooter Lone Ranger cap gun when I was a kid, and even that misfired as often as not. I had absolutely no way of knowing if the Luger would go off in my hands or not. I didn't know if I wanted to shoot Irvin, even by accident. I didn't know anything for certain.

Donny kept opening his mouth and closing it, catching a few random mosquitoes in the process. That wasn't doing any good to anyone as far as I could see.

"For Christ sake, Donny, say something."

He opened and closed his mouth one more time before finding a half a dozen useless words.

"I didn't mean to do it," Donny croaked.

I felt Irvin tense, like he was going to jump. I screwed the barrel a little tighter into his ear canal, breaking some of the soft pucker flesh. I hoped it was intimidating him, but he didn't look all that intimidated to me. I might as well have been squeegeeing a pussy willow Q-tip in his ear for all of the good it seemed to be doing me.

"Say something besides that, Donny," I begged. "Say something he'll listen to."

Donny started talking. "The woods. I was blueberry picking and burning ants with my magnifying glass. I didn't mean to start a fire. I didn't mean to burn it all down."

Holy Christ. He wasn't talking about the hotel fire, he was talking about the bush fire, way back when we were kids. He'd reached back into his memory and dredged up the ancient past.

"For shit's sake, Donny, that was years ago," I said. "What about the hotel fire?"

"Huh?" Donny asked.

It was good to have a vocabulary. I tried to put it to better use than I had so far, but Irvin beat me to the punch.

"You mean you didn't start the Railroad Hotel fire?" Irvin asked.

"I burned down all the trees," Donny said. "I didn't mean to. I was just playing."

"But what about the hotel?" Irvin kept digging.

"He didn't do it, Irvin," I said. "It was a misunderstanding. He's talking about burning down Jack Pine Stretch, for Christ sake. We only guessed he was talking about the hotel."

Irvin looked like the lights were going in his brain, one by one.

"We were guessing, do you get it? We were guessing about Donny and we were guessing about Tyree. We were wrong about Donny. That means maybe we were wrong about Tyree too."

It took a lot to get through to Irvin.

"Could be," he said.

I kept working at it.

"Focus, Donny. We are here for the hotel fire," I said. "How did it get started?"

"I don't know how it happened," Donny said. "I just don't know."

"Do you see?" I asked Irvin.

Irvin kept looking like he was chewing over it. I figured I'd better be safe.

"I'm keeping this," I said, pointing the Luger straight at Irvin. "I don't know if I'm going to use it or not. Don't fuck me with me Irvin. I'm just not in the mood for it right now."

"So what the hell are we going to do?" he asked.

"Same thing we set out to do," I said. "We're going up to that switch and we're going to scrape up whatever is left of Tyree and we're going to bury it. Isn't that right, Donny?"

Donny looked agreeable. If he'd had a tail he would have wagged it.

Irvin didn't look half so happy. He looked as if he'd love to tell me to go fuck a splintery knothole, just as soon as I let go of the Luger.

So I hung onto the Luger.

We walked up to the tracks; only by the time we got there Tyree was long gone.

9

It's easy to lose things. You can lose your car in a parking lot if you're not careful how much you drink at the party you were driving to. You can lose the remote beneath the couch cushions if you're not careful with how much you eat between commercials. You can lose your girlfriend and your wife, sometimes even at the same time. You can lose your dog, hell, you can even lose your mind if you think too hard about it, but losing a body is something else entirely.

The switch was still there. It had opened, now that the train had passed. The signal station, three hundred miles away, had automatically closed the circuit and opened the switch.

There was something clumped in the metal where

the switch had closed and reopened. It looked like a bit of crushed meat. Actually to me it looked an awful lot like the smoked meat slices you get in a those plastic boil-a-bags, only with a lot more ketchup.

I didn't want to look any closer.

"Well you got to hand it to Tyree," Irvin said. "He sure knows how to make his mark."

That did it. I shoved Irvin hard. While he was catching his footing I clocked him with the butt of the Luger, getting a good swing on it and putting my weight behind all of it. The Luger might have gone off, I suppose, but right about then I was pissed.

Irvin went down on one knee. I pointed the Luger and cocked it like a pro as if my hands suddenly knew what they had to do. I felt the spirit of a German SS Hauptsturmführer moving through my arm, hungry for a revenge-by-proxy on the verdammt Allies who had stormed over his homeland and eaten all of his bratwurst and sauerkraut.

I stared at Irvin. There was blood leaking from his scalp, but he didn't seem to mind that. He was staring just as hard as me. Something had changed between us. Right then and there I knew that whatever else went on tonight that Irvin and I just weren't ever going to look at each other the same way we used to.

"You want me and Donny to look away for a minute or two while you try real hard to go and fuck yourself, Irvin?" I asked, only this time I meant it.

Irvin kept staring at me, like he was committing every detail of me to memory. I kept the gun pointed straight at him, just in case he took it in his head to take a swing at me. Luger or not, Irvin was still nobody I wanted to fuck around with. Even on a good day he was a bad man.

"Where'd Tyree go?" Donny asked.

"Either that switch took his hand off at the wrist, or

the train did," Irvin said. "It looks to me like he crawled that way."

"Maybe he yanked himself free," Donny said. "That switch closed on his hand awful hard."

I tried to picture that. Tried to wrap my head around the kind of desperation it would take to rip your own hand off.

"Maybe the train ripped it off," Irvin suggested again, like he was trying to talk himself into it. "It looks like he crawled that way."

He pointed to the left of the track. I looked where he was pointing, turning the gun. He could have jumped me then, I suppose, but the two of us were busy staring at a path of blood glinting in the starlight.

There's always a trail if you look hard enough for something to follow along with.

10

Tyree must have crawled a long way into the darkness. Irvin, Donny and I had followed the blood trail for a good twenty minutes, stalking him down like a wounded deer but there was still no sign of him other than the long drag of burnt vermillion.

We kept at it. I wouldn't stand for anything else. We had to put this thing to a finish.

"There's no way he could have crawled this far," Irvin said. "We've missed him for sure."

"There's no way to know that for sure," I said. "You're just guessing."

"There's a lot of that going around," Irvin said.

Donny didn't say a thing. He just kept walking along with us, occasionally gingering his fingertips across his jaw line, right about where Irvin had hit him. Funny, how that was. You face a truck wreck, hand wrestle a bear to death, stage an execution and it's your best buddy who really leaves the mark.

I felt the dirt and debris crushing beneath my feet. Every step we took out here killed something. A leaf, a bug, a fern, it was all fair game. We stomped it all down flat, like a steamroller road crew from hell.

Nobody said a word. We just kept walking into the darkness, three not-so-wise-men stumbling through the black of the forest hunting down a trail of blood. I might as well have been a shadow of Irvin, him walking in front of me and me following blindly behind pointing the gun so that I felt in command of the whole situation. Donny trailed the two of us like a lag-along echo-ghost.

How far had Tyree crawled? Why hadn't he bled out yet? There's a hell of a lot of plumbing and pipe work in your average wrist. How much blood was there in one man?

I didn't know. I was only guessing.

The trail kept snailing out in front of us like a taunt. I wondered if somebody might not have been dragging him. That was possible. Might be it was just one of the track crew, or just some wandering woodsman who happened to be out for a two a.m. stroll through a moonless wooded stretch of jack pines. Might be it was a bum or a really big family of raccoons. Might be they'd found what was left of Tyree and were dragging him home for a game of one-handed crib. Stranger things had happened.

The mosquitoes were thick around us, their buzzing a constant hum, like power moving through the darkness, whirling nits of electrons swinging around some dark atom of guilt. I could hear something following us in the darkness in the woods beyond my sight. I could hear it pushing the branches aside and parting the shadows and snuffling through the underbrush. Whatever it was it sounded god-awful big. Maybe the bear had a buddy, only this sounded bigger than a bear. Bigger even than a moose.

Fuck. I was losing it. I needed some sleep. I needed a drink.

I needed to finish this.

I hung harder onto the Luger, welding my fingerprints into its machine-tooled grip. I told myself I could take care of everything. The memory of the SS trooper assured me that it was all right to just simply follow orders. I damned near believed it.

And then we found Tyree.

He was crawling through the woods, hauling himself along through the brackle and the underbrush, using his one good arm like he was attempting to swim the sidestroke through the dirt. His hand was completely torn off and he looked like he'd lost a hell of a lot more blood then he should have had in him in the first place.

"Holy fuck," Donny swore.

Irvin giggled. Right then and there I would have cheerfully shot the son of a bitch, except there was something hiding out beyond the darkness and the silence that I didn't want to wait for all by myself. I didn't think Donny or Tyree were going to be much of a help if whatever that was decided to come out of the darkness. Irvin, bastard or not, was a tough fuck-nut and I wanted him handy if something went down.

I knelt down beside Tyree, like I was kneeling beside a cocked-open bear trap. I could feel some kind of dark energy emanating from him, like the humming you feel in your bones if you stand too close to a power generator.

"You're okay," I said. "We're here."

I don't know how comforting that particular sentiment was, considering that we were the three assholes who had put him in this predicament in the first place but I just had to say something.

"I can't find my hand," Tyree said. His voice sounded like something inside of it had broken, like glass and those little tin ringer-thingy bells that you see on tricycles and little kid's bikes. "I've lost it somewhere."

I hauled my shirt off. The mosquitoes were going to have a fast food feast-out on my belly meat, but I didn't give a good goddamn. I tried to wrap the shirt around Tyree's wrist stump to bind it up. He kept waving the arm around, like a branch shimmying in the wind, flailing around like all of the bones in his arm had gone to rubber. It was like trying to splint up a broken Stretch Armstrong action doll with a couple of soggy popsicle sticks.

"Damn it, Tyree. Damn it. I'm so sorry."

I kept wrapping the shirt around the wound, but the damned thing kept coming loose. You couldn't really call what Tyree had a wound, anyway. It was something way bigger than a wound. It was like a door into his life, and everything was running out, and we were the three fuckers who had opened the door in the first place.

I felt somebody beside me. I looked around. It was Donny, kneeling like an altar boy at prayer.

"I'm sorry too, Tyree. I'm sorry we killed you."

He took out what he'd saved from the bear and pushed it onto Tyree's stump. I heard the bear meat suckling onto the wound like the pucker of a fat man hickeying onto a well cooked spare rib.

"Here," Donny said. "Take this. It'll give you strength."

I wasn't sure how that was supposed to make sense, but not a whole lot of this night was making much sense in hindsight. Of course hindsight was only good for looking out of your asshole and wasn't much of a replacement for a good pair of field glasses.

I wrapped the shirt around whatever Donny had torn from out of the bear and given to Tyree's arm, and it seemed to stick the shirt on solid, like the best kind of

Crazy Glue. I felt the shirt moving in and out in my hand, like the wound was breathing through the bit of bear.

"Here," a voice grumbled from above the three of us. For a moment I thought it was the bear, come back from the dead to set things right.

I looked up. Irvin was standing over us. He was holding out a pack of cigarettes like he was getting set to offer a smoke.

"There's got to be tobacco if you're making medicine with the dead."

He shook the cigarettes loose and crumpled them one by one, making a broken kind of circle about what was left of Tyree. I saw a fleck of the tobacco spackle onto the left of Tyree's lip. A part of me wanted to flick the damned thing away, but another part that knows enough not to whisper in church or whistle at a funeral told me to keep my hands the hell to myself.

"I'm sorry for killing you too, Tyree," Irvin said, and it felt like he really meant it.

Tyree's eyes sort of half-focused up towards Irvin. I could feel something between the two of them, like the two of them were chained in thin air.

"I didn't do it," Tyree whispered. "I didn't kill your brother, Irvin."

"I know you didn't," Irvin said. "I just wanted somebody to blame so bad that I looked around for anything in sight."

"It's all right," Tyree whispered. I had to lean closely to hear him. "Shit happens."

That last bit hit Irvin hard. It might have been easier if Tyree had just sworn at him or spit in his face. But letting go like that, letting go and not showing any sign of anger hit Irvin harder than a sixty car train wreck.

"Give me that pistol," Irvin said, taking it from me.

I don't think I could have stopped him if I'd wanted to. It was kind of irrevocable. It just had to be, you know what I'm saying? It was kind of like gravity and rain falling down. That gun just left my hands and passed into Irvin's, like it was something that just had to be.

I looked up at him, standing there over the three of us – me, Donny and Tyree. He could have shot us all, if he'd wanted to. He might even have been able to do it with one bullet, we were bunched up that close together.

Only he didn't.

He raised the pistol up towards the air.

"Goddamn you, God," he said low and gravelly, and then he fired three more shots straight up into the air. I don't know if he was trying to hit something or not.

"There's magic in threes," Irvin said. "There are three fates, and three sides to every story, and three stooges, depending on how you count."

I don't know if Irvin was conjuring or cursing.

"Give me that Luger back," I said.

Irvin looked at me. "You scared I'm going to shoot you?"

"I want to shoot one, too. For Tyree."

He handed it to me, butt first. "There are only two shots left."

"One's all I need," I said.

I held the Luger up to the sky. It felt heavier than it ought to, like it was freighted down with something a little more than bullets. Then I fired it, just once.

It seemed louder than before. Maybe my ears were just hearing it better.

It seemed to take forever for the sound of the single shot to fade away.

When the echo had vanished, Tyree had stopped breathing. I set the Luger down beside him. There was nothing there but the three of us standing in the darkness, listening to the mosquitoes buzz.

"We got to eat some of him, too," Irvin said.

I didn't argue. I lit a fire. Donny just watched.

Irvin got his hunting knife out.

"You want something from his leg?" he asked.

"I sure don't want rump roast," I answered.

Irvin finished carving. The whole proceeding had a kind of ceremonial feeling to it, like a last supper or a midnight church picnic. "Let's take our time and build us a good bed of coals and cook this up right."

"Daylight's coming soon," I pointed out.

Irvin just looked at me.

"I seen the light," he said. "Are you going anywhere too soon?"

I shook my head.

Irvin looked at Donny.

"Why don't you go on home, Donny. Somebody needs to get that truck back to the shop."

Donny stared. "I want to stay and eat with you."

Irvin shook his head.

"We'll eat some for you," Irvin said. "You run along now, and get that truck back, before I get pissed at you."

"You're always pissed, Irvin."

Irvin grinned at that.

"Not anymore," he said.

Donny wandered off. I watched him walking away. A part of me wondered if maybe he hadn't set the hotel fire. He hadn't really said that he didn't. You never could tell with Donny.

I'd be fucked if it mattered that much to me any more.

"You think he'll find his way back to the truck?" I asked.

"If he doesn't he can follow the track. One way or the other it'll lead him somewhere."

The fire was growing.

"Do you think he did it?" I asked. "Started the hotel fire?"

Irvin shrugged. "It doesn't matter that much,

anymore."

He looked at me like he was sizing me up.

"You don't have to stick around either," Irvin said. "This wasn't your idea."

I shrugged.

"I'm hungry," I said. "I'll stay and get my fill."

Irvin nodded.

We watched the fire. For a while we could hear the sounds of Donny crashing through the woods. Then, even that passed.

"Too bad we didn't bring us some marshmallows," Irvin said.

I laughed at that.

"So what do you think happened?" I asked.

"Happened with what?" Irvin asked.

"With the Hotel. What do you figure started the fire?"

Irvin looked out into the woods. I had the feeling he was looking at something, listening to it.

"Damned if I know," he said.

"Don't you even care?"

"Fuck," Irvin said. "Gilbert was always an asshole. I never did care much for him. He was just my brother, was all. He was someone I looked up to, because there wasn't anyone else around. And now there's nobody."

He stared out into the darkness, looking at something that I couldn't see.

"That's just how it is," Irvin said.

He picked up the Luger and pointed it straight at his skull, all business. "Shit happens, and then you die."

Before I could stop him he'd fired the last shot. I felt another baptismal spatter of warm jelly and bone bits slapping the other side of my face. If I'd been sitting a little closer I might have got caught by the bullet.

Irvin fell like a sack of meat with his legs still crossed Indian-style. He looked peaceful lying there, almost content.

I looked at him.

"If you think I'm eating your sorry ass, you've got another think coming," I said.

I added a bit more fuel to the fire and roasted a chunk of Tyree. I said my respects and chewed slowly. As I chewed I could hear the bear brains and Irvin's brains arguing back and forth across my skull bone, staking out their claim. I figured they each had an argument to share.

I added a few more sticks to the blaze.

The flames leapt higher, crawling out of the circle of the rocks and tobacco and into the hush of the dead pine needles.

I sat there quietly watching the flames grow, getting larger and larger until they reached out and touched everything.

Other books from Gray Friar Press

Poe's Progeny – An Anthology of Contemporary Stories Inspired by Classic Dark Fiction

- 30 original tales from the modern masters of horror

Bernie Herrmann's Manic Sextet

- 6 original novelettes

The Faculty of Terror by John L Probert

- A sublime film horror anthology in prose

Dark Corners by Stephen Volk

- A collection of short stories from the *Ghostwatch* and *Afterlife* screenwriter

Stains by Paul Finch

- Three novellas and five short stories from a modern master of horror

Dirty Prayers by Gary McMahon

- 25 short stories from a powerful new voice in horror

Rain by Conrad Williams

- A devastating novella from a writer at the height of his considerable powers

Printed in the United States
200053BV00007B/1-9/A